MW01519564

DEATH IN JERUSALEM

Also by John C. Boland

Donald McCarry mysteries

The Seventh Bearer
Brokered Death

Other novels

Rich Man's Blood
Easy Money

DEATH IN

A DONALD MCCARRY MYSTERY

JERUSALEM

JOHN C. BOLAND

ST. MARTIN'S PRESS NEW YORK

DESIGN BY JUDITH A. STAGNITTO

Library of Congress Cataloging-in-Publication Data

Boland, John C.
      Death in Jerusalem / John C. Boland.
          p.   cm.
      "A Thomas Dunne book."
      ISBN 0-312-10965-2 (hardcover)
      1. McCarry, Donald (Fictitious character)—Fiction.
    2. Stockbrokers—Israel—Fiction.   3. Americans—
Israel—Fiction.
      I. Title.
      PS3552.0575D43   1994   94-581
      813'.54—dc20   CIP

First Edition: July 1994

10 9 8 7 6 5 4 3 2 1

For Mira

and her flock of cops

and genial hosts Judy, Chesky, Joel, Marsha, Giora, Uzi, Leslie, August, and Pearl,

who are in no way responsible for the result

DEATH IN JERUSALEM

ONE

Harry Brickman thought I should see his house, which was twenty minutes outside the city. "No problem as long as we don't stop on the highway," he said, stuffing a small black machine pistol between the front seats. He had curly blond hair, a round pale face, stubby ears. "If we get forced into a ditch, you'll see what life is like for pioneers."

He had owned a villa, as he called it, near an Arab village for ten months and talked like a defender of Jerusalem in 1948.

"Jews can live wherever they want over here," he declared. "What do you say to that?"

"No neighborhood is safe."

"You're so right. Syria claims everything to the sea. I say my grandchildren will have villas in Damascus. Who's right?"

He was a bit of a nationalist, Harry Brickman was. But he was sincere in the role. When a war threatened, Harry left his desk at Morgenstern Ozick at the foot of Broadway, where the only incoming rounds were bonds he should

1

have ducked, and jumped the first plane to Tel Aviv. He'd gone twice under those circumstances since I'd known him. Last year, Harry'd had a good run shorting biotech stocks and had built his house. Now he made the eleven-hour flight every four weeks. The other partners at Morgenstern Ozick said Harry had better open a Jerusalem office.

He'd met me for breakfast at 8:15 on the hotel terrace, looking startlingly unfamiliar in a pink plaid shirt and rumpled khakis, with a black sweater around his neck because it was cool this high off the coastal plain. Without his usual navy suit and flashy tie, he looked less serious and more reliable, just an easygoing neighborhood guy.

We hadn't talked much business. He wanted to tell me about the Middle East's problems. "What did Koestler say? The Jews' struggle is the human predicament carried to its extreme?"

I hadn't read Koestler, and I didn't trust Harry's quotations, so I didn't say anything. I'd known him too long. He talked a lot about "the human predicament." The phrase explained away the contradictions in his own life. It excused his breaches with his children. It explained his lawsuits with ex-clients. It allowed him to take any political position that suited him.

He gunned the little Fiat along King David Street, joined the highway that went east. The road was wide and almost empty. There wasn't much business between Israel and its neighbors. Anything that could be traded had to be transshipped through Cyprus. "They fly stuff over there labeled Jaffa oranges, and it comes back as Holy Land citrus," Harry said. "It's crazy. But look who you're dealing with."

"The Jordanians?"

"No, I mean *us!* We're nuts. We help them pretend we aren't here. If it was me, they could eat Jaffa oranges or eat camel balls."

2

He was also a diplomat, Harry was. One reason he'd half-relocated, I suspected, was he had made so many enemies on Wall Street. One deal he'd had a hand in had brought securities regulators sniffing around the firm. They hadn't come on their own. Somebody had turned him in.

Barren hills lay ahead, more gray than brown, harsh in the slanting morning light. The previous afternoon, I'd taken a taxi up from Tel Aviv, past tree farms and cultivated fields that turned scrubby only on the steep climb to Jerusalem. We were about forty miles from the sea. The hills lying ahead looked as desolate as if they'd been a thousand miles from civilization. As we crested a ridge, Harry pointed to a Bedouin camp a few yards off the road. There was a ground-hugging tent watched over by tethered camels. No people were visible. At the base of the hill was a crossroads. "If we go that way," he said, jerking a thumb south, "we could follow the Dead Sea past Masada. Do you like heights?"

"Indifferent."

"Well, Masada is a mountain fortress. You get there by cable car."

"Oh."

"It's a shrine to Jewish obstinacy. You ought to see it."

"Isn't knowing you enough?"

He ignored me. "In 73 c.e., nine hundred and sixty men, women, and children killed themselves rather than fall into Roman hands. Actually, ten men drew lots to do the killing. The Romans said they were bandits. The road goes all the way down to Eilat. That's our Red Sea port. You go along the bay a couple of miles and you're in Jordan. Drive fifteen minutes in the opposite direction and you're in Egypt. The Mideast is one small town, and the neighbors all hate each other."

He shrugged at the road south, which looked as wide as a bicycle path, and turned left.

Along the roadside was a small hut manned by two young soldiers. Harry started to wave to them, then slammed on the brakes and popped out. "Hey, guys, the Arab Legion's coming down the pass!"

The soldiers looked at one another without smiling. They might have been eighteen or nineteen years old. One of them took his left foot down from a Coca-Cola crate, left the right foot elevated. Their expressions were readable. It was early in the day and already they'd met an American asshole.

"Is there any trouble ahead?" Harry asked.

One of the youngsters shrugged. The other didn't bother. The one who shrugged said, "Are you going into Jericho?"

"Shomrim Tsion," Harry said. "I live there."

They gave each other looks that said, *He would.*

"You don't have an Intifada car," the other soldier said. "You should have an Intifada car."

"It's a rental . . . *his*," he said, pointing at me. "My BMW's in the shop."

"There hasn't been trouble since Sunday," the first soldier said. He picked up a tattered issue of *Penthouse* and ignored us.

Harry Brickman climbed back into the driver's seat. "The most that would happen is some kid might throw a rock," he said, forcing the gears. "Unless they get the windshield, that's Avis's worry."

"What's an Intifada car?"

"Steel mesh screens over the glass. We don't need it. People from Shomrim Tsion make the drive a couple times a week. The village kids don't mess with a convoy full of trigger-happy settlers."

We weren't a convoy. I thought about pointing that out.

4

If I did, Harry would have gotten his kick. Half the fun of inviting an outsider home, I suspected, lay in getting him worked up. I'd known Harry for eight years, had watched him and his two colleagues run their investment partnerships from eight million to forty-something, and thought I knew his appetite for risk. He didn't normally hang around where there was trouble. For traders like Harry, "long-term" is a week. Short-term is twenty minutes. They can unload eighty percent of their stock positions at noon and be back in at 2:30.

A few miles past the guard station, we passed two kids at the edge of a village, tending a soft drink stand that had no customers. They wore kaffiyas and were a couple of years younger than the soldiers but otherwise didn't look much different. I said to Harry, "How do you tell the Jews from the Muslims?"

He glanced into the mirror. "It's tougher than that. Those kids aren't Muslim, they're Christians. That's a Christian Arab village." For a moment he was silent and his face was still, as if he saw a real-life human predicament he couldn't resolve. Deciding to be cheerful, he patted the machine pistol. "Here's how I tell the difference. I put on my *kippa* and go for a walk. If they shoot at me or throw rocks, they aren't Jews. If they yell *'Allah akhbar!'* when they do it, they aren't Christians. If they just shout something stupid like *'Fatah!'* they could be Muslims but probably are Christians."

He turned to me, and the car swerved onto the shoulder. "How do you tell the Jews in the stock market?"

"If a broker takes a point from both the buyer and the seller, he's Jewish."

"That's a nasty stereotype," Harry said. "He could be a Baptist trying to improve himself. If a guy *pays* a point when he buys and a point when he sells, then you've got something. He's a putz, so not Jewish."

5

"He could be a Muslim."

"No, a dunce like that's gonna be a New Testament baby. Did you visit the souk?"

He meant the Arab shops in Jerusalem's Old City. I had and I got his point. "They're good bargainers," I said.

"Now, if you'd gone through the Jaffa Gate, you could have been fleeced by Armenians. They're good, too, but they're Christians. The exception proves the rule. There aren't many Armenians on Wall Street."

"So how do I recognize Jews in the stock market?"

"If the guy's named Goldfarb, you just know," Harry said. He was having fun.

We went round a bend in the road, and a hundred feet ahead there were three men standing in our way. They wore ski masks, green T-shirts and khakis, and they were pointing large fancy-looking rifles at us.

"For instance," Harry said, "they're not Goldfarbs."

His foot jittered between the brake and the accelerator. He finally hit the brake and we skidded to a stop, tail swishing around so we were broadside to the road. That put Harry's door closer than mine to the three men. It was probably what discouraged him from picking up the machine pistol. That and the way the man on the right stepped forward and fired a burst into the hood of the Fiat.

When the shooting stopped, I brought my arms down from my face and lifted my head. Harry sat still. He hadn't covered his face. He said, "I think they want us to get out."

I tried the door handle. Nobody shot me. I opened the door a crack, and when nobody responded, I stepped onto the road. The surface felt mushy, but that was because my knees didn't want to lock. We were in a small depression, with neither a village nor Bedouin tents in sight.

Harry was getting out on his side as the three men advanced. They were five feet from him. All were large and hairy-armed. Behind them, a jeep pulled out of a wadi and sped in close. The driver also wore a mask.

Harry had a bright idea. He shouted at them, "Hey, you assholes—we're American!"

The man nearest to Harry Brickman swung his rifle into Harry's face, and as he crumpled a boot found his groin. The gunman looked across the car's roof at me. He brought his rifle into line with his eye. He didn't say anything.

He didn't shoot me. I didn't object.

They bundled Harry Brickman into the jeep and drove away.

TWO

My office at Magee & Temple was three blocks north of Harry Brickman's headquarters. Both occupied older buildings at the bottom of Manhattan, where in May the stone walls and pavements radiated heat and garbage smells. The main difference in our accommodations was that Magee & Temple had owned its building since J. P. Morgan *père* was a pup, while Harry's firm, Morgenstern Ozick Management, sublet a couple of thousand square feet that had belonged to Drexel Burnham. We might never have run into each other except that after listening to Harry explain his stock market tactics one evening at the Portfolio Club, I offered to buy him lunch if he fed me some business. Running portfolios that got emptied out and restocked three times a year, Harry and his partners had a lot of commissions to spread around the town's brokers. I lived for commissions the way busboys live for tips. The commissions financed my pursuit of everything else that mattered.

Unfortunately, Harry's idea of a fair commission rate was about one-sixth of my idea. So we didn't do much business, but we got to know each other. Our views of the stock market and human nature were compatible. Not identical, but we approached matters from a similar perspective and could talk shorthand on most topics.

One exception was Israel. Harry Brickman was an ardent Zionist, probably because of all the other things he couldn't believe in. Despite my surname McCarry, I couldn't remember the last time I'd wondered or cared about what was happening in Ireland.

"You would if your people had been cast out of Ireland two thousand years ago," Harry said.

"No, I wouldn't." If they were like my old man, the first McCarrys had been run out of quite a few places, including the better taverns. Detained in a few places, too, anywhere stealing pigs violated local custom.

"You're a man with no heart," Harry said.

"Who knocks commissions down to two cents?"

"I do my best for my partners. What's the crime?" He waved a hand that brought a gold Rolex flash. The market had closed twenty minutes ago, and he had dropped by Magee & Temple's building with a dinner invitation. One of his investors had some cash that couldn't go into the partnership for tax reasons. Could I use a new account—three million, give or take a few weeks' interest—and could I promise not to pick the client's pocket in that this person was a close friend of Harry Brickman's? I told him I had a special commission structure for his friends.

He wouldn't tell me anything about the client. We walked through the quitting time pandemonium up to the restaurant on Dey Street. The captain greeted Harry as if he'd bought the place. The air conditioning was turned high enough to keep the beer mugs frosted. We got a table a few feet from the door to the bar. The captain didn't think so much of Harry after all. I didn't mind. The revelers were harmonizing in the same key. They'd all made a bundle today. Any afternoon the Dow jumps a percent and a half, brokers swear they owned nothing but the thirty stocks in the average, no sleepy little dogs that wouldn't bark if you kicked them, no losers headed south in an up market, and sure as hell no short positions. *"Closed all my shorts at a profit yesterday, Jimbo, just before she took off." "Closed mine on Tuesday, Bobster, and I call that foresight." "My clients love me." "Mine, too, and so's my wife. It's your turn to buy."*

Harry ordered a bottle of pricey bordeaux, glanced at his watch. He looked up at me. "Would you rather start with three or four martinis?"

We started with martinis, while the wine sat and breathed cigar fumes. Midway through the second round, Harry's client arrived, and the talk turned from money in general to the particular money of one Gideon Larkis, Esquire. The talk consisted mostly of Harry assuring Larkis he'd known me since we were bar mitzvahed together and I never lost clients more than they could afford. Gideon Larkis, Esquire, inspected me with the enthusiasm a liver-eater has for a plateful of bean sprouts.

"What's the reason you can't go into Harry's partnerships?" I asked.

"Divorce," the counselor said. He was sickly pale, with hair that was almost jet black. His eyes were deepset, his cheeks hollow. He looked as if he had achieved a runner's leanness without ever seeing the sun. "Linda knows about Morgenstern Ozick. She knows to the dime how much we've got there. I need something the bitch doesn't know about."

Harry piped up. "Third Wife Syndrome. Gideon's lost all his old romanticism."

"I never had any," Gideon Larkis said, and from his dark

eyes I believed him. "I was just too horny. If it had a cunt, I had to poke it. Then *marry* it. It's ruined my life."

"It could have got you chased out of the Bronx Zoo," I said.

He stared at me. Being on the receiving end of his affections—or attentions, anyway—entitled a wife to anything she could get.

"Gideon sues people for us," Harry said. "He's got the best plaintiff's record in town. The competition would rather settle than face him in court. As for this little fiddle, Gideon'll have to disclose the account, of course. But we thought you might do some reverse repos and create some quick losses."

"That recover in a couple of years," Larkis added.

I picked up the menu to have something to stare at besides Larkis. What they wanted, if it was just meant to dupe poor Mrs. Larkis, was fraudulent. But the transactions would also have tax implications. Fictitious losses would lower Larkis's tax bill. The IRS was generally even less forgiving than cast-off spouses.

Watching a three-million-dollar account flutter away, I said, "I'll see what Compliance says we can do." The munchkins in Magee & Temple's compliance department hated imaginative transactions the way a nun hates upside-down sex. When possible, I avoided asking them.

Larkis was chewing something side to side. Bread was the only thing on the table. Reaching for another dinner roll, he told Harry: "Your friend's a pussy."

Harry kept his eyes on his menu. "Anything you want to do, Gideon, has to go through somebody's compliance department."

Larkis glanced from one of us to the other. I waited for him to tell us he was a lawyer and it was legal if he said so.

—

11

Instead he put his napkin on his plate. "You're right, Harry. I'm gonna have to leave you honest gentlemen. There's business I forgot about. Say hello to your partners."

Harry watched him go and said, "I didn't know you were so fussy, chum."

"How long has he been your lawyer?"

"About a year. Warren's close to him." Warren Morgenstern was one of his partners. "I didn't figure you could do what he wants. He'll find someone."

"You may need a new lawyer."

Harry shrugged. "He's tough. That's what we need. These days managing money means filing lawsuits. We've got three going right now. Guys running companies think they can steal from stockholders. They get a smart lawyer to show them how. We get a smart lawyer to try to spoil their fun. It's getting to where I don't want to buy into something unless we control it."

I told the waiter who'd drifted up that I would have the filet.

"I'm sorry you didn't take his business," Harry said.

"No you're not. You went through the motions for him."

He grinned. "So I don't like lawyers. Are you still seeing that Kimball girl?"

It was a change of subject. She wasn't a lawyer. "Off and on," I said.

"Still trying to rope in her old man's money?"

"Charlie Kimball has his own brokers. He puts the spurs to them, and they jump."

"Me, I never liked Waspy women."

"I hear the Israeli women are nice."

"Knockouts. Why'd I have to marry young? You should come along next time. We'll find you a good Sabra girl."

I looked at him.

"Reform," he said, "very Reform. Most of them aren't religious."

"What would I do with a girlfriend in Israel?"

"So you see her once or twice a year." He shrugged. "You should come over anyway. Explore business prospects."

"I didn't think there were any."

"They got problems, for sure. What do you expect? The place was founded by socialists. The labor federation owns a quarter of the industry, and the government owns more than a fifth. Is that a ticket for success? You fire a bus driver and the country goes on strike. But it's getting better. They're sure as hell open to foreign investment. We've been putting a little money into this and that over there. If one thing works, we'll get an annual return of forty percent."

"Good luck," I said.

"I'll give you something closer to home," he said. "Viscount Industries, trades in the pinks, four to a half. We've got a full position in the main partnership, so help yourself."

"Why should I want to?"

"No, you're supposed to say 'How much can I buy without disturbing the market?' To that one, the answer's maybe ten thousand shares, no more. But if you're patient, get your bid in, you might pick up a bigger piece."

"You haven't answered my question. Why do I want to? Do you control this one?"

"No, but management's a bunch of born-agains who're too honest to steal. Good people. Two generations work there now. As for 'why,' they got a real, tangible book value of about eleven dollars a share. You could sell the company tomorrow morning for north of fourteen."

"I couldn't. I don't run the thing. Does the second generation want to sell?"

"That's not the reason you buy the stock. They print T-shirts—you know, cartoon characters, baseball teams—and have been earning okay money, sixty cents two years ago, eighty the past year. This year it'll be a dollar-forty. They signed a big contract with pro football. Next year, they'll do two bucks, and the stock'll be thirty-five or forty. And it'll be listed on the New York Stock Exchange. That comes later this summer."

People tout stocks to me nine hours a day. Every money manager has his pet story. By the time I hear them, the stocks usually have doubled or tripled and the tout is hoping to sell his shares to me. I kicked Harry's present in the haunch and lifted a lip to inspect the teeth. "Why is it so cheap?" I said.

"It's been forgotten. Came out of a bankrupt conglomerate six years ago. Creditors got stock they've been selling ever since. Let me break your heart. When I started buying in December, the price was seventy-five cents." He beamed at his own stock-picking skill and poured me another glass of his expensive wine.

It didn't quite break my heart. But it put a little ache in it for all the money I could have made if Harry Brickman had told me the story in December. The hurt didn't ease when I reminded myself he would never have let the company's name slip while he was buying. He wouldn't want the competition.

We weren't *that* good friends.

My *loft's lights* were on, and Stacy Kimball was draining pasta. I have a fascination with watching an elegant woman perform menial chores. Cooking, to be sure, needn't be menial. In some hands, it's even considered an art form. In Stacy's, "menial" is a generous description. The product of her efforts would never inspire a young boy to leave home to join the pursuit of truth and beauty. He might leave home to hang out with Stacy.

I stood and watched. A nicely shaped, well-bred, russet-haired young woman with houses in Connecticut and Maine can't make herself look completely awkward. But pasta cooked to the consistency of melting cheese doesn't lend itself to graceful draining. The mass hit the colander like white Jello without the quiver. She looked around brightly and asked me, "Clam sauce or tomato?"

Stacy Kimball is not given to domestic niceties. A few generations of too much money purges the genes of inclinations to cook homey meals, clean toilets or darn anybody's socks. My antennae twitched a warning.

I hadn't expected to find her here. Yesterday we hadn't been speaking, after she had run out of arguments about why the life of a stockbroker was too trivial for a man of my talents. When she set out to improve me, it was useless to point out that selling stocks suited me perfectly. Whole generations of McCarrys had studied poaching, pignapping and check kiting so Donald McCarry would inherit a knack for selling stocks. My forebears' acquired skills hadn't missed much. Selling bikinis to Eskimos would have been useful. Magee & Temple had floated a few stock deals that were about as helpful to capital preservation as a thong bottom was to an Aleut's suntan.

"Aren't you disappointed in yourself?" she'd asked last night.

I would be disappointed, I said, when I couldn't pay the mortgage on the loft. A mortgage, I added, was something she had never had to worry about.

15

"I pay a mortgage," she said. She did, too, on a cozy co-operative apartment on Central Park West.

"But you've never had to worry about it," I said. "You've got a safety net."

The safety net was Tracer Minerals Corporation, and her father, Charlie Kimball, controlled more than half the voting stock and ran the company. Or, more exactly, he sat by the telephone on his porch on Waubeeka Island and ran the people who ran the company.

While I looked for a bottle of wine, Stacy spilled cold tomato sauce onto the pasta and fed the combination into the microwave. After a few seconds, the clear glass door became opaque with steam.

Grateful for Harry's steak, I said, "Are you, um, very hungry?"

She smiled. "I could get by with a nibble, if you've got that in mind."

There was a *splat* against the microwave door.

She heard it, went over and said, "Oh, shit!" Pasta entrails hung from the inside of the door. As a kid she had probably microwaved at least one hamster. Just to see. She was rich but not very proper. She gave me a look. "What do we do about this?"

"We could turn it on high for twenty minutes, see if it's self-cleaning." Before she jumped on that thought, I said, "Or we could wait for the cleaning lady."

"You don't *have* a cleaning lady.

I tore off a wad of paper towels. "Here you go then."

"But this blouse is silk. It cost—" She thought better of telling me. If we ever got to the point where I had to keep her in silk blouses, the price tags had better come as a surprise.

"I'll hold it."

She gave a Joan of Arc glance at the bare rafters, shed the

16

blouse. The bra was silk, too, and she knew she didn't need it for aesthetic reasons. She hung it on my arm, bound her hair back with an elastic band, and looked down at herself. "Shame about the skirt."

"Well . . ."

"And in that case . . ."

"You're not trying to distract me?"

"No. Just think of me as the kitchen maid."

She turned to the job at hand. I told myself to ignore my suspicions and enjoy the sight. Before the microwave was back to its pristine state, we got into a wrestling match that ended halfway onto the butcher block kitchen island. After that, she kissed me heartily while rubbing a counter crease out of her backside. If all life were a cooking school, we'd have gotten on fine.

She didn't have much to say in the shower, held her thoughts as I toweled her hair, kept the day's agenda to herself as we walked a block to SoHo's nicest Italian dump. She was pretty certain that silent and enigmatic went together. Someone had convinced her that anybody who sits in silence with a thoughtful frown is presumed to be thinking.

After a while, she got impatient when I hadn't coaxed her thoughts out of her. She gave me a wide, sails-up smile. "How would you feel, sweetheart," she said, "about living in London?"

I'd have a hard time fitting in anywhere that takes its airs seriously. Or where damp weather is called fortifying. Or where haute cuisine means boiled potatoes and Spam. Otherwise, the idea sounded good. "Magee & Temple doesn't have a London office," I said, knowing that wouldn't end it. "What brings this on, anyway?"

"I heard there's an opening for someone with American investment experience."

She had no more contact with the financial world's

grapevine than I had with Buckingham Palace's. I said, "What kind of opening?"

"It's on a trading desk, executing orders for portfolio managers, and I know that sounds like a step down"—it was more like nose-diving down an entire staircase—"but it's terrifically responsible and would be a kind of fast track to—"

"Tell Charlie no thanks."

"You wouldn't be working for Daddy."

"Tell him no thanks anyway." If he wasn't in the forefront, Charlie Kimball would be only a few steps into the background. And that wasn't far enough.

"The thing you should think about," she said evenly, "is what you're going to be doing in ten years."

Every morning I asked myself just that question. I didn't like the answer that came back, but it was probably the right one. McCarry would be selling Magee & Temple's finest line of designer stock certificates, a fad suitable for every pocketbook, a fashion statement for every retirement portfolio, a dud for every season. If not Magee & Temple's merchandise, then some other brokerage firm's. I was thirty-nine years old and had never held a job apart from selling stocks. When I wasn't too scrupulous, I made a decent living. More than a New York bus driver, less than a Gideon Larkis. I kept my clients out of the worst-smelling deals our corporate finance department dreamed up and avoided customers who wanted to break more than one law at a time. Most mornings I could shave without wincing at the clever fellow staring back at me. Nor with much urge to pat him on the back. Not wincing wasn't enough.

Stacy picked up her wine glass. "You look awfully glum, Donald."

"Thinking about the future does that."

"I'm sorry I suggested it."

"The future can't be too grim if it includes you but doesn't include your father."

"That's gallant." Her admiration for her dad wasn't of the intensity that would have gotten Freud excited. At exclamatory moments in bed, she never cried "Daddy!" Her admiration flowed from Charlie's good-natured charm and his mastery of circumstance. He was a small, tanned man with short white hair, who played easygoing tennis, poured drinks that were neither stingy nor extravagant, and kept the external threats to his family at a safe distance. In Stacy's heart, he was a man of character. In my estimation, he had money and understood the things it could buy: among them, an appearance of grace that wage earners could only envy.

He knew better than to trust the family portfolio to me, but he'd never discouraged his daughter as she tried to get us together in an employer-employee relationship. From Charlie's point of view, it would be perfect. It would be a short-lived relationship, and once he booted me from the family payroll I might bounce out of Stacy's life as well.

That might indeed end the affair. Stacy found road accidents as interesting as the next person, but she didn't bring the victims home to bed. And she would never blame Charlie for the damage.

He was smarter than his daughter realized, or admitted, and more devious. I preferred a boss who was neither smart nor devious, but I could live with devious if he needed help lacing his shoes.

That let Charlie out on two counts. He would never be my boss and probably, if I admitted the truth, never a relative-by-marriage, unless he saw a major angle he could exploit. Our last meeting had been so cordial my neck hairs rose. On the broad lawn of his Connecticut island house, Charlie in white Daks and blazer clapped my shoulder—

19

sidewise, he wasn't tall enough to come over the top—said he regretted I hadn't visited every afternoon that spring, presided over a cheerful cold lunch served on the porch, and with a lab dissector's precision pumped me for information about a Wall Street banker I'd never heard of. Even when he realized he'd wasted a good lunch, he remained friendly. "So Donald, are there any stocks I should buy?"

I said no because there weren't and he wasn't interested anyway.

He'd wanted information on an investment banker. He didn't need an investment banker's services. So there was another reason for his interest. On the drive back to the city, I wondered for whom he was doing his snooping. Or rather, for what government agency. He had informal ties throughout the federal and state bureaucracies. The connections were useful if you controlled a company with widely dispersed interests. If one of Tracer's mines had a small environmental problem, someone might remember that Charlie had done a favor for a deputy secretary. And somebody else might be told that Tracer's mess was minor, trivial really, and not worth the enforcement effort when so many bigger problems demanded attention.

The lunch had been two weeks ago, and his gamesmanship was still vivid in my mind. I'd been watching the newspapers casually for word that the banker had acquired official problems. I wasn't about to kid myself about Charlie.

"I could always try money management," I said.

"McCarry Investment Management," Stacy said, trying out the sound. "Not bad."

"It has cachet. You could continue to be seen with me."

She didn't know that down-at-heels money management firms were as common as mom-and-pop groceries, with similar mortality rates. Bringing brokerage clients over

20

wouldn't be easy. People felt comfortable with blue-veined Magee & Temple—comfortable and safe, imagining that patrician fingers didn't grab wallets and roll grandmothers down the stairs.

Harry Brickman's pet stock was down an eighth the next afternoon. I bought ten thousand shares. An hour later, Harry messengered over Viscount's financial statements, which showed the company had been tearing up the rug in the latest three months. Impressed, I picked up another ten thousand just before the market closed. I could call the company and see if Harry's high expectations matched their own. But that was about as thorough as I would get. Viscount Industries was based in St. Louis. Visiting them was out of the question.

Besides which, what would I see but T-shirts?

THREE

Life *at Magee* & Temple lost its last shimmer of glory when Mad Max brought down orders to sell a movie deal that would have stunk if the promoters had had *Gone With the Wind* in the can. The underwriters, of whom Magee & Temple was second behind Shearson, got commissions, fees and expenses that added up to eight percent of the total amount raised. The three bandits who had put the company together got salaries, origination fees (if they ever shared a movie idea with the company), production fees (if they ever got a project off the ground), and a percentage of gross receipts (if the brainstorm ever flashed onto a movie screen). Way down below in the coal cellars, where the chumps who bought the shares lived, all you could hear was the sound of water dripping.

If stockbrokers ran in packs, grabbing necklaces off ladies in good restaurants, they would put us in jail. (Or perhaps not, if we stuck to New York.) Because we operated out of a rosewood and stained-glass office with ornate ceiling moldings trimmed in Wedgwood blue, the ladies brought their necklaces and checkbooks and threw themselves across our desks, sobbing, "Thanks for the opportunity."

Harry Brickman's stock, on the other hand, was at nine and a half, up about one hundred twenty-five percent in three months. My clients and I had one hundred sixty-three thousand shares, average cost four and seven-eighths, and I wished I had bought more. When I called Harry to thank him, I was hoping he would drop another name.

"It's not doing too bad, is it?" he said. "My advice, stay with this one. Your next stock, you never know. This one—forty in twelve months. Why switch?"

"I'll stay with Viscount," I promised. I would, too, until I smelled Harry Brickman or his friends selling. We traded worthless opinions on the market. We consoled one another on the sorry state of New York City. He confided that Gideon Larkis had been arrested trying to leave the country with a suitcase full of money.

"The cops think he was laundering cash for Colombians," Harry said. "He was just trying to get it out of Linda's reach."

"You can be his witness."

"I never heard of the guy." He hemmed, as if getting an idea. "Gideon was going in on one deal with us, pint-sized, nothing like what he was trying to hide from Mrs. Larkis. Right now everything he owns has a court seal on it, which leaves us an opening. It's a little sexier than T-shirts. We're also getting in earlier. This is just the third round of financing; the first two were tiny. Would any of your clients go for a private placement?"

"It's kind of exotic," I said. I wanted to be sold, maybe even tickled under the chin, before I said no. The people for whom I had bought Viscount Industries would spring for a hamster breeding ranch if I told them to. McCarry was on a roll. He could do no wrong, until a few trades soured and he got demoted back to idiot. Putting clients into a private placement could get me there in one step. Little companies grasping for capital have a way of turning tits up as soon as your check clears. The rare good deals—the start-ups with a fighting chance of giving you back twenty times your money—get quietly set aside by two or three bespoke-suited gents having lobster bisque in Morgan's coziest dining room. If a deal bounces down all those flights of stairs to reach the retail brokers, it tells you something. It says everybody along the way with any smarts looked at it, sniffed, poked, and ultimately decided to keep his money in his pocket.

"You're wondering, has this been shopped around?" Harry Brickman said. "Let me answer you this way. I put it together myself. Our partnerships have eighty percent and will be in for their full share of this round. Apart from that, I've shown it to two people. Gideon was the first, because Warren wanted him in. When he got into trouble, I took it to another person—you would recognize the name—a person to whom I owe a favor that can never be fully repaid. For his own reasons, he declined to participate. You would be number three."

He'd gotten very formal as he spoke. On the other end of the line, a nice rabbi was helping me reason through one of life's puzzles. And if, on the side, the rabbi owned a deli that was loaded with pastrami that was turning green, shouldn't he share his problem with a friend?

"Harry—" I said.

"I'm not pushing this, my friend. You take a look, you don't like it, that's okay."

I smelled month-old pastrami. "Harry, why are you putting me third on your list?"

"I'll tell you the truth. I like the way you bought the Viscount Industries shares. How many have you and your people got? Two hundred thousand? And you didn't budge the price except at the end. I watched it. You would push a little, then pull back, charming more stock out on the way down than you bought on the way up. So I tell myself, he's an Irish *momzer* but maybe we can do business."

"Okay, I'll take a look."

"You're doing me no favor."

"If I don't like what I see—"

"You don't buy."

"All right."

"You'll thank us for the opportunity."

Meg *Sorkin was* at her work station, in the center of a blue-carpeted foyer, framed by brokers' offices and the elevators. Four of us occupied the suite on this end of the eighteenth floor. The east corner office belonged to Art Bradshaw, a thirty-some-year veteran of Magee & Temple. I seldom saw him, except for a blurred glimpse, about once a week, of a hunched gray figure hurrying past Meg's desk to his four telephone lines. He could juggle lines holding three prospective customers while he sold a fourth a package of oil wells or strip shopping centers, guaranteed to pay eight percent a year until the driller or the tenants went broke. Timmy Upham and Isaiah Stern had the other offices. The four of us shared Meg's secretarial skills. Only Timmy got to take her to hotels.

All three of my colleagues' office doors were closed. It was 10:30 on a Monday morning, and nobody was hanging out at the coffee pot. Meg was on the telephone, settled back comfortably, dark hair spread over the top of her chair, legs stretched out, ankles crossed. If I wanted a letter typed, I would have to pull the fire alarm. Fortunately I don't write many letters.

The center door of the elevators sprang open. Before I could duck, the manager spotted me. He had a tiny grin, like a pitcher who has turned suddenly and stares eye-to-eye with a runner who is about three strides too far off first. The smile says, *I can nail you any time I want, but I will enjoy it more if you try to run.* Max Oberfeld tucked his hands into his trouser pockets. The trousers were navy with a chalk stripe. His shirt had narrow red stripes. The necktie would have been stripes, too, if they made them running up and down instead of diagonal on ties. Somebody had told Mad Max that stripes make short men look taller. He was trying to stretch five foot four to fill his image of himself, which was on the order of six three. He walked as if he were tall and rangy, with a little forward tilt and a back-and-forth sway, Lou Gehrig headed to the batter's box, Will Kane bearing down the dusty street toward the gunslingers. I wondered what Max Oberfeld's personality would have been like if he'd never had to wish for tall parents' genes.

His grin widened as much as the little face could accommodate. But he was disappointed I hadn't tried to hide.

"Glad to see you've sold your quota this morning, Donald," he said. He had a small voice that stretched words lengthwise, adding irony and a palette of colors but coming out, unbeknownst to Max, more Liberace than Gary Cooper.

"Good morning, Max."

"You *have* sold your quota?"

"We don't have quotas, Max. We fit each investment to the client."

"You're talking like a shoe salesman. In case you've forgotten, you're on Wall Street. Just letting you have a desk here costs Magee & Temple money. They ask me to check in periodically to see if you're worth the rent."

If they let him, Max would come up in heels, a leather

apron, and a whip to urge us on. On the eighteenth floor, he was known to everyone except Meg as Oberführer, more widely as Mad Max. Meg referred to him only as Mr. Oberfeld. Art Bradshaw and Timmy Upham had hired her and trained her, but she planned to work on the eighteenth floor long after the last of us was gone.

Max spun in a pirouette, his glance sweeping over the closed doors, over one secretary/assistant reading trade reports into the telephone (what the person on the other end thought of the end of gossip and the commencement of financial gibberish was anybody's guess) and settled on the knot of my necktie. He never looked up. In place of faces, he saw an array of neckties, stubbly chins, and goiters.

"Speaking of desks, I'm looking for a place to park one of our new employees. Mr. Wacker recruited this one himself directly from the alma mater. . . ."

"That would be Harrow?" If our chairman Thornton Wacker adopted any more Anglicisms, he would need a green card.

"Always the wiseass, McCarry. Our lad, Howard Harslip, distinguished himself at Yale by managing a speculative account for several classmen. Very impressive results—much better than you've done. You didn't even *go* to Yale."

"Neither did you."

As if I hadn't interrupted, he said, "So I was thinking— you boys take up a lot of space to limited effect. I'll bet I could squeeze Howard in up here."

"I thought rocket scientists went straight to trading or corporate finance."

"Howard's degree is in philosophy. Math never touched his innocent mind. He just happens to have a nose for profitable investments." Max ran a dainty finger along one eyebrow, as if he didn't quite believe it himself. It wouldn't be the first time Magee & Temple let someone with a nose for good investments cross its threshold, not quite the first time, but close.

"You don't want to plant him up here," I said. "We'll infect him with our losing ways."

"Not to mention your laziness. Bradshaw is the only one of you who pays his light bill. Stern spends the day reading the Koran. Upham's busy bonking the help. What's your excuse?"

I could have said moral reservations. But it was too high-toned a thought for either of us.

When I didn't answer, he swayed forward on the balls of his feet. Gregory Peck inspecting the hair follicles of lesser men. "What I'm going to do is break up this little country club. One of the three losers up here is going to give up his office space. I'm not sure which of you it'll be. Any suggestions?"

"No."

"There may be space down on sixteen for the evicted party. Then again, maybe not. I'll decide after I see how each of you does with Film City Screen Partners. I haven't noticed many shares sold."

I stared at him. "You say there may be space on sixteen or may not. What's that mean?"

"It means we may reduce staff. That seems pretty clear to me. How about you?"

"It's clear."

"Good. I wonder if your colleagues are in so I can give them the news."

He went away, and I closed the door. My office didn't have much of a homey look or feel. I'd had half a dozen nineteenth-century bond certificates framed. They still had all their original coupons, which was my measure of how fast things could go sour once other people had your money. There was personal clutter on my desk—a photo of Stacy Kimball and her sister in Paris, a banker's lamp my father had given me, a Mets coffee mug full of pens and lint. Otherwise the place was as impersonal as a telephone booth. It wouldn't take them long to move me out. Howard Harslip could be settled in before lunch.

Behind my desk was a shelf loaded with the glossy sales brochures for Film City Screen Partners and a half dozen other offerings in which Magee & Temple was part of the selling syndicate. They warned you, I thought. They called them *syndicated* deals. If brokers had names ending in vowels, people would get suspicious. But how could a firm with a name like Grosvenor Brothers or Harriman, Hill & Drew be anything but gentlemen? Even Magee & Temple, because the Magee had come over early enough to have lost the immigrant taint, was supposed to have been nice to old ladies.

I sat down and punched up the symbol for Viscount Industries. The shares had gotten listed on the stock exchange, just as Harry Brickman had promised. The numbers flashed up 9 1/4—9 5/8. The first was the price at which somebody was willing to buy, in this case, the screen noted on the side, four hundred shares. The latter was the price at which another someone was willing to sell six hundred. I called Cheryl down on the trading desk and told her to go in to buy four hundred shares for my own account at nine and a quarter. I was getting in line behind the other buyer. Not an aggressive move. If a large, impatient seller came in, though, I might pick up the stock at that price. It was better than buying at nine and five-eighths and then having a seller knock the price down.

I thumbed through the preliminary prospectus on Film City Screen Partners. The preliminary prospectus provides a lot of information about the company, but it doesn't have the final offering price filled in. Good soldiers like me were supposed to be lining up buy orders from their customers. If they can stir up a lot of interest, the price will get nudged up before the deal is done. They call the preliminary prospectus a red herring. That's because a paragraph of disclaimers is printed sidewise on the cover in red. And if they sit around too long, the deals get an odor like week-old carp.

I tried to think of a client I didn't like, who deserved Film City Screen Partners. My clients weren't all saints. They paid for trades late. Sometimes their checks bounced. They disowned purchases, saying the stupid broker didn't hear right. They listened to my best stock idea and then bought a hundred shares from me before going to a firm charging cut-rate commissions, where they bought five thousand. They demanded new copies of tax statements at 4:30 P.M. on April 14.

Not all saints.

But I couldn't think of one who deserved a piece of this partnership.

I rolled the red herring into a cylinder, flung it like a baton at the trash basket, and wondered what life on the sixteenth floor—or at another firm—would be like.

Harry Brickman's office was festooned with more electronic screens than a space launch center. There were all the machines you would expect to find supplying news and prices to an active trader: an ADP, a Bridge, a Bloomberg, but there were also a couple I couldn't identify, with prices marching across the screen following symbols I didn't recognize. European or Far East markets, I supposed.

Ben Ozick was on the desk, talking into a headset as he inspected an electronically generated chart on the ADP.

There was no sign of Harry. A glass-paned door stood partly open to a side office. A gray-haired man sat at an old steel desk, feet up and shoeless, a newspaper spread on his elongated lap. Warren Morgenstern.

Still no sign of Harry.

The office was grimly functional. No stained-glass panels or gilded scrollwork or carved mantels. The directors' meeting room at Magee & Temple had all three, along with leather sofas and inlaid side tables supporting green-shaded lamps. The mantel could absorb a visiting client's attention for a half-hour. On either side, standing four feet tall, pygmy warriors in three-quarters relief presented spears and menacing faces. The only ornamentation in Morgenstern Ozick's suite was a large serigraph that Harry had brought back from Jerusalem. The scene showed an open gate in an ancient stone wall that had flowers sprouting from crannies and lions above the opening.

Ben Ozick got off the line and shouted, "Are you one of the pigeons for Agritech?"

Before I could answer, Harry Brickman came in. "It's Ben's fate to be a skeptic," he said to me, in an apologetic tone.

"And it's Harry's to be gullible enough for two people," Ozick replied.

"His money's in," Harry told me. "He worries lest it should work out."

His partner leaned back, fingers locked in front of him. He was tall and thin, balding, with features that looked like they had shrunk. He wore a bold striped shirt, a flowered tie, braided leather suspenders. "Speaking of working out," he said, "we are up nine hundred thousand on the Nikkei options. The Jap market looks like it could take another pasting tomorrow. Should we let it ride?"

"What does Warren think?"

"The Nikkei could hit twelve thousand by September, in which case the puts double from here."

Harry's shrug told him it was his decision. Harry sidled into his chair, dug into a stack of papers at the exact middle, and pulled out a few stapled pages that he sailed down the desk at me. It was an offering circular for shares in something called Agritech Consultants Limited, of Jerusalem, Israel. There were no photos, no fancy type. The thing looked as though it had been put together on a typewriter and then photocopied. Beneath the company's name were the number of shares being offered and the designation Mezzanine Financing.

"Is it a real company?" I said. You can't insult someone who's trying to sell you something.

"Young, vibrant, with a great future."

"Any revenue—or is that all in the future?"

"A little. The first contract is under way. We figure the company becomes self-supporting in eighteen months. Meantime, this infusion of capital lets them ramp up the marketing."

"How long will the money last?"

"There may be one more financing, but it will come at a higher price. This is the last chance to get in cheap-cheap."

I mumbled something.

Ben Ozick said, "No guts, no glory—tell him that, Harry."

Harry nodded. "Like the guy says. But like *I* said, you should feel comfortable or not do it. We're not closing for three weeks, so you've got time to think."

"And your money's in it?" I asked Ozick, just to be sure.

He seemed embarrassed. "Afraid so."

"And Ben's never bought an Israel bond," Harry said.

"Neither have you," his partner replied.

"My father used to."

"Mine, too. But we're a more sophisticated generation."

Nine days later I was in Israel.

Harry had repeated his offhand invitation. I'd have told him to forget it except that the walls were closing in. Stacy had set me up for dinner with Charlie Kimball. Mad Max had decreed a meeting of all the troops. If I was getting the sack, I didn't want to be on hand for Max's ceremony. Or for dinner with Charlie. Being out of town wasn't a good enough excuse for ducking either engagement. Being out of the country, researching a rare opportunity for clients, was beyond reproach. Or at least *I* was beyond reproach, literally, by six thousand miles.

The trip wasn't totally a sham. Agritech Consultants intrigued me. Not enough to climb onto a plane. Not enough that I was likely to invest much. But I'd read enough of the offering circular to get Harry's point. The market for the company's technical services was wide open. If Agritech clicked, its early investors could make many times their money.

"It's a plain vanilla speculation," Harry said.

Which made Harry, by implication, a plain vanilla speculator. I never quite bought his pitch on the stock. I shouldn't have bought his pitch on himself.

Plain vanilla speculators don't get hijacked.

FOUR

I *stood on* the highway beside the shot-up car.

The engine ticked like a hall clock. It wouldn't cool much. The sun was high above the eastern hills that Harry had told me were in Jordan. Its heat penetrated the transparent desert air like a laser. The weight of the light was like a fat man's hands pushing down on my shoulders. It was like a hammer blow on the back of my head. A man left exposed out here would bow quickly to the sun's mastery, and soon curl up as the drying muscles and tendons contracted.

My watch indicated it had been five minutes since Harry and his abductors drove away. I wasn't due to die from the heat just yet. Or even later. There were the Arab boys a mile behind me, tending their soft drink stand.

Several things commended that direction. The prospect of a cold Kinley was foremost. But also the border guards were back that way. And the jeep with Harry had gone the other direction.

I decided to move the car off the road. Someone hurtling around the bend from Jerusalem wouldn't have time to react. I walked around to the driver's side and climbed in. The engine screamed a complaint, hammered four times, and quit. I shifted the gear to neutral and pushed the Fiat to the shoulder.

Harry's gun remained between the seats. Taking it with me seemed pointless. I didn't know how to operate the thing. On the other hand, anyone I came across wouldn't know that. And with nothing else to occupy my attention, I might figure the mechanism out. The thing was all matte black, small and square-edged, not very heavy. I looked for something that might be a safety, couldn't find one. There was a braided strap that I wrapped around my hand. If I swung the thing just so, it could be mistaken for an ugly little purse.

There we were, McCarry armed for combat.

And fortunately not a masked man in sight.

The young captain of the Israeli Defense Forces was named Arik and spoke in a high-pitched Brooklyn accent. He had a small round face, short-trimmed black hair, olive skin, and an air of good-natured confidence. He handed me another orange soda. I was sitting in the back of his jeep, disarmed and sweating.

"You were really stupid to walk along the highway," he said. *"Especially* packing a gun you can't fire."

"So you've said. If I could, I'd have driven."

Two armored trucks howled past on the road. They were the fourth and fifth I'd counted in fifteen minutes. Helicopters had arrived first, sweeping down the highway like heavy-nosed bloodhounds almost as soon as Arik had radioed the alarm.

He leaned against the jeep. "Tell me again why you were there."

"Harry wanted me to see his villa."

"He is a friend of yours?"

"That's a matter of opinion."

"He'd pissed you off?"

And so on. We'd gone over it twice already. Why was I in Israel? What was the company called Agritech Consultants? Where was I from in the United States? What was my employer's name? And did I know Chaim Davidowicz, who was also a stockbroker, working with Merrill, right down on Liberty Street, with whom Arik had gone to Hebrew school in Borough Park?

When had my plane arrived in Israel? What had been the flight number? Wasn't it great flying on El Al? *And why was I in Israel?*

Much less about the four men in masks and green T-shirts.

"Have you seen them on American television?" he asked, as if American television was something he'd only heard about in Borough Park. His Brooklynese had taken on the local habit of making every statement a question, except the questions, which came out flat.

I said, "Have I seen who on television?"

"That is the garb of Palestinian terrorists. It is shown on American television."

It was the garb of Irish terrorists, for all I knew, not to mention Italian terrorists, Basque terrorists, and guys knocking over pizza shops on Staten Island.

"So what?" I said.

"I am trying to determine the events," he said, a little stiffly. "How long have you been in Israel?"

"Twenty-four hours."

"Brickman's abductors—what did they say?"

"I don't remember exactly."

"What language did they speak?"

36

Now he had stumped me. I took a gulp of soda, stared down at the two Arab kids who were bargaining with a soldier for a plastic bag full of melons. What language? Almost certainly Arabic, I thought. Playing the confrontation back in my mind, I wasn't sure. When had they said anything in Arabic? Their most eloquent statements had been a burst of gunfire, which amounted to *"Stop or you're dead!"* in any tongue, and a gunstock smashed into Harry's face, meaning *"Don't fuck with us."* They hadn't shouted anything at Harry that meant get his ass over to the jeep. They hadn't screamed at me the Arabic equivalent of stand pat and keep your hands up. They hadn't cried out anything that sounded like slogans—*"Death to stockbrokers!"* or *"Bugger the Zionists!"*

"They didn't say anything," I said.

"That is your recollection?"

"Yes."

"Nothing?"

"Not a word."

A radio barked. I couldn't identify the language but guessed Hebrew.

The young captain spoke to the caller, then said to me, "We will go take a look."

His three comrades piled into the back of the jeep, one lugging melons. Arik climbed in beside the driver. We drove the mile to the bend in the road. Another jeep sat a hundred yards beyond my Fiat. Three soldiers lounged with their floppy green hats pulled down. We pulled abreast of them, and Arik spoke to one of the soldiers. The man was a little older. His glance flicked at me, not a long look.

Arik and the other man staged a small contest over who could take longer climbing out of his jeep and getting both feet onto the road, legs shaken straight, butts unscrunched, backs stretched. The outcome was too close to call. Arik beckoned to me. "We'll eyeball your car—is that okay?"

"Eyeball away," I said. "I haven't counted the bullet holes. You're welcome to do so."

"Come help us."

A hundred yards is a long walk in dry, broiling heat. The two soldiers didn't seem to mind. They stopped at the half-way point and waited for me to catch up. After that, Arik walked with a hand on my shoulder. He made the same small talk. "So, how do you like Israel?"

"It's hot," I said, "and the roads aren't safe."

The other man said something that brought a chuckle from Arik. "Like New York in August."

We were near the Fiat when they stopped. Not right on top of it, but within ten feet. It looked worse than the average parked car in New York. Maybe that depended on your neighborhood. Avis wouldn't be ecstatic unless they had some fiddle with the government for cars lost running the Territories' gantlet.

Hands in his pockets, the other soldier walked this way and that, noting the damage, the paint job, the wax job.

"This is your car?" Arik said.

"It belongs to Avis."

"It is the car you and Mr. Brickman were driving?"

He wanted precision, so I joined the game. "Mr. Brickman was driving. I was riding."

"You had rented the car, but he was driving." He seemed to be staring at a spot on my forehead. I didn't think I had a spot there. The thought that he *thought* I had one made me uneasy. He was getting around to something, the way the merchants in the souk got around to price. It was round about—"*You're from America? You like our city? Do you find anything in my shop to be worthy of interest?*" The step after that was to block the door until the visitor agreed that yes, this final price would put poor Yousir and his brother out of business and therefore had to be fair—and yes, the visitor would open his wallet right now.

Captain Arik didn't move his gaze from the curious blemish on my forehead. "How did it happen that your friend was driving?"

"He knew the way. We were going to his villa. Remember?"

"I remember that is what you told me," he said mildly. "Shall we examine your automobile? Does it look as it did when you left it?"

"No," I said—and he halted in midstep, "it looks dirtier."

Which was true. A film of dust had settled over the white body and the glass.

"But otherwise?"

"Otherwise, shot up—no different."

The two Israelis glanced at each other. Arik bent over, planting his palms on his thighs, and put his head through the open driver's window. He turned slowly, inspecting as much of the interior as he could from that frozen stance. The older man stood several feet back, looking at the bullet-holed hood and fender. They were interested in Avis's car, and they were wary, as if—

Sometimes I'm slow on the uptake. They'd left the jeeps a football field away. They'd walked me down here, almost arm-in-arm, and neither of them had laid a hand on the Fiat. When Arik pulled his head clear, I said, "Do you get a lot of booby-trapped cars?"

I expected him to jump. Instead, he turned his round face toward me and said, "A few. It is bad for tourism. Do you know anything about bomb-making?"

I almost said no, but he was beginning to annoy me. Actually, he had been annoying me ever since arriving at the soft drink stand. The kids who let me use their uncle's telephone had at least sold me an orange soda cheaper than they came at the King David. While we waited for the army, they berated the Mets. The Cubs would take the division. What did I think? Arik had popped for a soda, but his conversation wasn't so impractical.

"I only set off bombs at the stock exchange," I said.

He considered the possibility I meant it. But I had come along to the car too willingly. Apparently I didn't look suicidal.

"Does the motor turn?" he asked.

"It didn't an hour ago."

"Why don't you push it onto the other side of the road, which has a better shoulder."

The shoulder on this side looked about the same, but I said, "Okay."

When I glanced around, they were walking away and had covered almost half the distance to the jeeps. Maybe they were going to bring a jeep down to do the pushing. Right.

I reached for the car door and froze. I looked from the retreating soldiers to the car. From the car to the soldiers. They weren't quite fast-marching, but they weren't pausing to count pebbles.

I felt like someone had poured a handful of ice cubes down my pants. All of a sudden, very uptight.

I touched a finger to the dust on the door and the glass. Got down on my belly and looked around the axles and the fuel tank. Got up, brushed off my hands. I opened the car door, slipped the gear and the brake, and urged the little car in a tight half-circle from one side of the road to the other. I smelled oil and saw a dribbling trail of black spatters had followed me across the road. The car wasn't going anywhere under its own power.

40

I left the key under the floor mat and collected the paper-work. Then I sat in the driver's seat. It was brutally hot. The passenger compartment was the size of a steam cabinet. There was nothing to give off steam except my body, and I could feel the moisture being sucked from my flesh. It wouldn't take long—less than a day—before the fellow resting in the hot tin box became as desiccated as the husk of a fly.

A jeep stopped in front of me, and Arik got out. He sauntered over and I said to him, *"Boom!"*

He didn't jump.

"Did you expect it to blow up," I asked, "or just figure there was an off chance?"

He shrugged elaborately. "One never knows."

Trying to keep a tremor out of my voice, I agreed, "One never does."

"Get in. We have another stop to make."

They let me ride in Arik's jeep. The road climbed, and the scenery remained barren: lots of rock, worn hills that too many of God's armies had marched across, nothing you could call a tree until we were on the outskirts of the new town. Shomrim Tsion wasn't much prettier than the surrounding hills. The houses were built of concrete block, some layered with smooth stucco. It was hard to tell which houses were occupied. Not many had glass in the windows. A couple that didn't have glass had kids looking out. The buildings wrapped around the upper slopes of a hill that commanded the neighboring valleys. If there were villages down there, they blended into the pale brown, pocked faces of the slopes.

"Is this the settlement?" I asked.

Nobody in the jeep replied. We were near enough to the town that I began to catch the flavor of life on the frontier, as Harry called it. It didn't look inviting. At the roadside, a

---

hundred feet from the first building, two white sedans were parked along with a large, open-backed truck. A man with a narrow gray beard and a black snap-brimmed hat sat on the fender of one car, knees drawn up, a small book open in one hand and a rifle a few inches from the other hand. He wore a white shirt, black trousers with a fringe of strings hanging from the side. In the back of the truck, elbows on the roof, stood a large young man with a full beard and a wide-brimmed straw hat. If an attack came, the protocol must be to put the truck across the road as a barrier and start shooting. There were no shoulders on the newly paved road for the first two hundred yards of ascent, until the road reached the men.

No waves were exchanged as we rolled past.

Over his shoulder, Arik noticed my expression and said, "It is a very religious community, and there have been incidents."

"Attacks by Arabs?"

"Rock throwing by Arabs, a few gasoline bombs, those things all the time, you know? But one of the settlers shot an old Bedouin last month. We arrested him, and there are hard feelings. Personally, I think it is good to have the enemy afraid."

Past the first line of houses, fruit trees were visible, even ornamental bushes. Farther along, as the street curved, a few houses on a grander scale appeared. Not exactly mansions but better than the neighbors' snug digs. The jeeps swung into an unpaved driveway in front of something that looked like a cross between an American ranch house and a one-storey professional building. When Harry talked villa, I pictured something Mediterranean or Italianate. Whether this style was California or New Jersey industrial park was a hard call.

A soldier standing at the front door shook his head. Two women in military gear came out of the house behind him. One called out something to one of Arik's men, who grinned and waved the bag of melons.

"Nobody home," Arik said, "but we will look."

Harry hadn't put much furniture in. There was a mattress on a platform, a table, and a couple of chairs. No sofa, no book cases, no china closet, not even a quotation terminal, a computer linkup, or a fax machine. No fax because no telephone. It was a long way short of seaside living in Antibes. The thing that had drawn him here must have been deeply felt. . . .

I caught myself on the verge of buying Harry's version of Harry.

Or he had expected to make a lot of money.

That was more like it. That was my kind of thinking. If you could make it worth my while, I could stand a few months in monk's quarters in a dry, dangerous place that didn't even have a 7-Eleven on the corner. Or a decent restaurant. Or a neighborhood bar. Or a video palace with every Gene Autry movie. Or even a stock quote machine. I wouldn't like it, but I could do it. Maybe, if the payoff was big enough. Nostalgia for the eternal homeland wouldn't enter into it.

If that aspect mattered to Harry, the place must have seemed less grim.

The house still wasn't what I'd been expecting. English editions of the *Jerusalem Post* were stacked near the front room's director's chairs. A table was loaded with business papers, some with Morgenstern Ozick's letterhead. Maybe he was taking his partners up on opening a Jerusalem office.

One of Arik's men opened a closet door. A two-foot-high mound of newspapers collapsed. The sole of an athletic shoe was partly visible. The head of a tennis racket was more intuited than seen. A few shirts and a couple of pairs of khaki trousers swayed on hangers.

A television set, or a CD player, would have been nice.

What had he done at night?

He'd told me the Sabra girls were knockouts. He probably hadn't told his wife, Karen.

"Do you see anything unusual?" Arik had come up beside me.

"No. It's a real palace."

He didn't answer.

"What did you expect?" I said.

"Nothing, nothing," he said in his high, singsong. "It is just that the terrorists do not usually kidnap people. The organizations are well funded, so they have no need of ransoms. When they come upon Jews, they kill them. Except usually we kill them before they get the chance."

"I don't follow."

"They did not kill your friend on the highway. They did not kill you. Assuming we do not find his body in a wadi, it means they have a reason."

"He's pretty well heeled."

"So, this could be an impoverished splinter group. That is possible. What is the name again of the Israeli company?"

"Agritech Consultants. They're in Jerusalem." I had learned that much last night. "Do you think they'll get a ransom demand?"

He shrugged with his whole body. Who could say?

"But you think he'll turn up in a ditch?" I said.

"We will see. Cheski will give you a ride back to Jerusalem."

* * *

Somehow it had gotten to be three in the afternoon. Cheski drove me to the front door of the King David and dropped me off. I walked up three flights of broad curving stairs where the carpet was getting a little ratty and turned the room's air conditioning on high. I showered and came out wearing the hotel's bathrobe and took the coward's way out on the next part. I didn't know Karen Brickman. It was eight in the morning in New York, and Ben Ozick was at his desk.

He let me tell him about four words before coming unglued. After a few minutes of his screaming, a calmer voice came on.

"This is Warren Morgenstern. Who the hell is this?"

I told him and repeated what I'd told Ben Ozick. He let me finish before saying, "Oh my God. Does Karen know?"

Someone in Arik's chain of command might have notified the embassy, who might get around to having someone in the State Department call her. I didn't know what the government's drill was when a citizen got stolen.

"Oh, my God," Warren Morgenstern said again. "I'll have to call her. Is there someone over there who'll have more information?"

"I don't know. It just happened. Rather, I just got cut loose. They might have briefed someone at Agritech, in case there's a ransom demand."

"If they're holding Harry, he might have them contact you," Morgenstern said.

I hadn't thought of that. Now that I did, I didn't like the prospect of four Arabs in masks "contacting" me.

"If they do," Harry's partner went on, "let us know right away. Take down our home telephone numbers. If they want money, we can raise it. We can wire it to you at Bank Leumi and—"

I cut him off. "The Israelis may not approve of paying off terrorists."

"Which means, from now on, a certain amount of discretion on your part would be helpful."

"I'll keep you posted," I said, and hung up before he came up with an idea that would get me arrested.

FIVE

I *walked down* to Avis with the bad news, came back and had a swim in the King David's pool. The sun had angled behind the trees, and I had the garden and pool almost to myself. An English mother was getting the worse of a struggle with two toddlers in water wings. A lean, deeply tanned man who looked somehow like a soldier on leave swam laps with the ferocious concentration of a hunter. I toweled off on the pool apron as a younger, taller, and fitter man came down the path to the water and said something to the lap swimmer. The newcomer chuckled to himself as the older man kept swimming. He said something again, to no more effect. He wasn't speaking English or Hebrew, I was pretty sure. Maybe Russian.

I was hunting up a soft drink from the concession stand when a man in a white jacket came down the steps between walls of flowering hibiscus. He checked out the alternatives and hurried over to me. "Mr. McCarry, sir?" He held out a small tray, which bore a buff envelope. I replaced the envelope with two shekel coins. The message inside was neatly printed on hotel stationery:

Join me on the terrace.
Sennesh

The name meant nothing. From my position I couldn't see much of the terrace except a section of columned rail and yellow umbrella tops. I followed the path up to the terrace steps, went up them two at a time. A waiter gave me a dirty look: a sign at the foot of the stairway warned swimmers off the terrace. On the other hand, it was the cocktail hour and only two of the tables were taken. One table had a family of five around it. The other was occupied by a woman with her face turned away. I glanced at the doorway to the inside lounge. The waiter hovered there, daring me.

The woman was staring through a picket line of tall trees at the back of the property. Between the bare trunks, you could see glimpses of the Old City's fortified walls, catching the evening sun across an intervening valley. She had her chin resting on her palm. Coming closer, I could see the angle made by the supporting arm. A long braided rope of black hair wound down the back of a tan blouse.

"Excuse me," I said, "are you—"

Her head came around. "Sit down. We haven't much time."

She didn't offer me a hand to shake. She hooked her fingers together on the table, like a vice president about to hear how things had gotten botched. Her fingers were long and dark with neatly manicured nails. Her arms had the dusky sheen of a Mediterranean evening. The face held traces of everyone who had ever walked, or sailed, or rolled across

48

the neighborhood in a chariot: a prominent straight nose, close-set brown eyes, round cheeks, a wide, thin mouth. She leaned into the table. "I work with Dov. The army told us about Brickman."

"Who is Dov?"

"Dov Levy," she said, and I was supposed to answer "Of course." I didn't. My expression told her she hadn't helped much. She said, "Dov Levy is president of Agritech Consultants."

I said, "Oh."

"I'm Miss Sennesh."

I said "Oh" again.

"Dov is worried about Brickman." That made sense. Brickman was the chief money bags. She added, without much of a break in her voice, "I am worried, too."

Harry had said the Sabra girls were pretty. Most of the ones I had come across of Miss Sennesh's age—early twenties, I guessed—were wearing army boots and carrying rifles. Even when the uniforms were snug, the rifles weren't a come-on, unless you were into that sort of thing. Miss Sennesh's tan shirt fitted snugly enough to bring an Arab army to its knees, or at least distract them, and I wondered if she had had that effect on Harry.

The glance she flicked at me was to see how much she'd given away. Otherwise she was looking for the waiter. I waved him over and asked her, "Do you want something to drink?"

"A Gold Star, please."

I ordered two Gold Stars. The table with the kids was getting large palettes with scoops of eight or nine different colored ice creams. Miss Sennesh eyed them with disconsolate lust.

"Go ahead," I said.

She shook her head. "You haven't seen the prices. Besides, it all goes here." She patted herself on a hip held in a short navy skirt. It looked trim enough.

I changed the subject. "The military said if the Arabs had planned to kill Harry, they'd have done so on the spot. Along with me. That means he's probably okay. We may have to come up with a ransom."

She shook her head. "It does not usually work that way in Israel. Could you pay a ransom if one were demanded?"

"Harry's associates could—a modest one," I added. There was no point in broadcasting their wealth. No point, either, in mentioning that Harry's family could put up a hefty payment. If Harry had been playing grab ass, Miss Sennesh wouldn't want to hear about Karen Brickman and the kid.

She went back to staring at the Old City's walls. "If Hezbollah has Brickman, they will kill him even if someone pays."

"If who has him?"

"Hezbollah. The 'Party of God.' It is an Islamic fundamentalist movement. Their terrorists infiltrate from Lebanon, or try to; we kill most of them." She let her reverie run down. The oversized bottles of Gold Star beer arrived, and half a glass began to restore her. "It could have been Hamas; they, too, are Muslim fanatics."

"What about the PLO?"

"They are now 'moderates,' officially," she said, putting a cupboard full of hate into the word *moderates*. "They deputize others to do their killing."

"I see."

"Brickman said you are an investor. Do you intend to invest in our company?"

I didn't want to give her more bad news. But it was probably better than kidding her and her colleagues along. If

Harry didn't turn up, it wasn't likely Agritech Consultants would be seeing more of Morgenstern Ozick's money, never mind mine. It had been Harry's project. "I came to look, not buy," I said.

"You mean you aren't going to invest in us?"

"It's not likely."

"Oh. . . ." The energy ran out of her again. She polished off the beer and said, "You should not decide until you have met with Dov Levy. He is excited about Agritech, and his emotions are contagious."

"I don't think there's much point," I said. My return flight wasn't for two days. I couldn't move it up and duck out while Harry was missing. At least not while he was freshly missing. I didn't know what the experience was in Israel, but in other parts of the Mideast people who were abducted tended to stay gone a long time. Or turn up in vacant lots with messages around their necks. A cheerful thought.

And I had thought people played rough on Wall Street.

Well, they do, I told myself. They just leave the machine guns home.

"You come all this way and do not want to meet the president of Agritech?" She seemed more puzzled than offended. "You must see him just to let Dov know everything that happened when you were with Brickman. There may be something you forgot to tell the army. It could be very important."

"I'll be glad to talk to Dov Levy about that," I said. "I'm just not—"

"Just not a buyer. That is understood. I will tell him not to try to sell you anything. Wait here."

She jumped up and strode across the terrace. I noticed a nice flex of navy-clad haunch, envied Harry a little if he had a friendly arrangement thousands of miles from where he could be pestered, pressured, or otherwise put upon. I wondered if Miss Sennesh's pillow talk included little hints to Harry that his career was pointless, his future empty, and he should join up with Daddy, who owned the biggest fish meal plant on the Gulf of Eilat. He'd been commuting for less than a year, and it took time for a woman to get enough in charge to set about the male improvement project.

In any case, I was assuming a lot. A little catch in Miss Sennesh's throat didn't have to mean anything.

I glanced out at the trees. The sun had left the Old City walls. For an unpleasant moment, I thought of hundreds of tiny apartments where wives were putting the supper pot on and plotting tonight's installment of "Yitzak, you must close the pointless stupid shop which keeps us alive but is beneath you and set to improving yourself—study dentistry; Cohen's nephew is a dentist and gets a lot of respect."

Perhaps it didn't work the same way in every culture. Perhaps Ali had sold the wife who started that routine to the camel caravan's trader, who needed brothel workers for Khartoum.

I got the waiter to bring me another beer. Dusk was coming out of the trees, rising on a scented breeze from the garden, and a few other tables had filled up. The customers looked about evenly divided between Israelis and visitors. The visitors dressed a little better and sat a little straighter. One table across the terrace had a crowd of at least ten gathered. A television actor I half recognized and a large, white-haired woman seemed to be competing for the right to hold court.

When she came back, Miss Sennesh saw me watching and gave a little shake of her elegant nose. "They are American Jews. Their organizations send them over, endless groups, to tell us how we should run our country. They daydream about retiring to Tel Aviv or Jerusalem, if it could be just like New York City or Chicago. None of them talks about retiring to a desert kibbutz, where there is work to be done." She stopped herself, bounced a couple of times to get comfortable on the iron chair. "You did not order me a beer. I will drink yours while you get dressed, and then I will try again to reach Dov Levy."

"It really isn't necessary this evening," I said.

"You may remember something important this evening."

I went upstairs, showered, put on fresh slacks, a striped shirt, and a blazer. Even that was too stodgy. I hadn't seen a necktie since getting off the plane, and not many jackets. Five telephone messages had come in: two a half hour apart from Warren Morgenstern, one from Meg at my office, and one each from the American Embassy and the Israeli National Police. There was nothing more I could tell Harry's partners. If Meg wanted to report that my desk had been moved out, the news of Max's revenge could wait. So could the Embassy spin doctors. I called the police number, listened to the answer, and hung up. My colleague Timmy Upham had taught me how to deal with phone calls that didn't promise business. You put them into one of three categories: calls not to be returned today, those not to be returned tomorrow, those not to be returned at all. He advocated skipping categories one and two.

Miss Sennesh had finished our beer and had gotten a glass of wine. I sat down, trying to remember the exact department name the police operator had given. I said, "Do you know what the Yaman is?"

"Ya-*mam*," she corrected. "It is a very important unit that combats terrorism. Where did you hear the name?"

"I read it." The anti-terrorism squad could have its turn at me tomorrow.

"We have a large population of potential hostiles," she

─

53

said. "Not counting the people in Judea, Samaria, and Gaza, sixteen percent of Israeli citizens are Arabs. They vote, they are represented in the Knesset, and some serve in the army if they choose. They live in Israel by choice, you understand. If they felt as free, or as safe, in Lebanon, or Syria, or Jordan, or Egypt, or Saudia, they would live in those places, would they not?"

"If you say so."

"In all those countries, there are only a handful of Jews. Our people are banned, in fact, in Jordan and Saudia." She stared at me as if she had made a point and I had missed it. "That tells you where people are freer and safer."

"What does it say about terrorism?"

"I was coming to that. Some of our population is motivated by myths of Arab nationalism. They view other Arabs as brothers and Jews as invaders who one day will be driven into the sea. So we have a problem. If there is another war, some people think we would lose. They are wrong, but it is a problem."

Her face was brighter than it had been. I didn't know whether it was distance from the topic of Harry, or enthusiasm for the topic of subversion. Or, for that matter, the terrace's electric lights could be responsible, or the alcohol she had consumed.

When she got up, she was perfectly steady. "Perhaps Dov is home now."

She disappeared, and I watched the Americans have a wine tasting. The actor held up a glass of claret and called down the length of the table, thereby alerting most of the terrace as well, "The nose is a little thin, Joel." The white-haired, heavy-set woman consulted with a small, baldish man in a double-breasted blazer. They held their glasses under their noses, swirled, looked at each other again, and nodded to the actor. I couldn't quite place him. I knew I'd seen him on television, but I couldn't remember the roles. He called to Joel: "Young, but drinkable." This time Joel nodded without consulting.

Miss Sennesh was a long time in returning. The crowd at the distant table expanded and took over two adjacent, smaller tables. They were passing another bottle. Someone toward the railing—not the actor—said, "This one's grape juice."

Miss Sennesh arrived as one of the tasters knocked a bottle onto the stone floor.

She looked over her shoulder. "They are getting drunk on Israeli wine," she said, as if it were impossible to understand. "I reached Dov's wife. He is not due for ninety minutes. I could come back then. I am hungry."

"So am I. Why don't we let Dov Levy wait until tomorrow?"

"No." She was adamant.

"All right. Can we get dinner here?"

"We could, but it is expensive. Agritech is not—"

"My treat." It might forestall a sales pitch on Agritech's behalf.

"Thank you. But we can do better nearby. It is just across the street, the Emca."

The Emca turned out to be the YMCA, which occupied an Ottoman fortress rising behind a deep lawn and flower beds. Miss Sennesh pulled my arm as we crossed King David Street.

"It looks impressive," I said, "but maybe not for dinner."

"You will see."

We got a table on the patio, between citrus trees. A bottle

of Golan Heights wine lifted Miss Sennesh's spirits. If Dov Levy had time, he could round up additional investors, she declared. Agritech would survive.

"I don't understand exactly what Agritech does," I said. I had a general idea: the company's consultants sold their agricultural expertise to other countries. But that was Harry's version. I wondered what hers would be.

"Mainly we work in the less-developed countries," she said. "There are a lot of things we've learned to grow under harsh conditions in Israel that could help them with their economies."

"What sort of things?"

"Many vegetables, melons. There has been much research in desert farming."

"And you can export that knowledge?"

"We need a separate license for each country. And there are some things we can't export, because the government believes they are too important or because we do not have a license from the inventor."

"How many projects are underway?"

"We've got one team in the field, north of Addis Ababa. Doctor Weizman is there, teaching desert agriculture, with Yigal and Jilly."

"How does Agritech get paid? I didn't think Ethiopia was buying much except guns."

"We don't get paid by the government. But we've got a contract with them. If we install one of our methods in a village, we get ten percent of the increased production for the first three years, then five percent for two years, then nothing. If production doesn't improve, we get nothing. If production declines in any year, the decrease is deducted from our next year's fee."

"You have to be sure of what you're doing," I observed. "A couple of bad years and you owe them money."

She took the last remark seriously. "That can't happen. The worst outcome, under our contract, is we end up not making any money. And if we improve things for a few years before there is trouble, Agritech gets to keep its royalties to that point. We couldn't take all the crop risk, because you never know when there might be a drought. Or a war."

What she'd told me explained why Agritech needed infusions of cash. I didn't know how long it took to get a project going at a particular locale. But prior to anyone's signing on, there would have to be demonstrations, and proving the effectiveness of an agricultural technique would take time. Even if you went from prototype to production without a hitch, it would be at least two or three years before any payments were due to Agritech. Meanwhile, Harry's clients' money was out there growing melons in the desert.

I wondered what had possessed him. If you wanted to pour money onto the stony ground and pray a crop sprang forth, there was no shortage of people in the States who would take your contributions. That would do nothing, of course, for a fellow burning with Zionist spirit.

A young woman with her hair in a prim bun brought menu cards. I eyed mine skeptically. The specialty seemed to be steak. Harry had warned me off Israeli beef. "The cattle are stringy," he said.

"Order the filet," Miss Sennesh said. "And another bottle of wine."

The steak was superb, and the wine was okay. The Golan Heights winery had imported an experienced vintner from France. That explained that, she thought. How to explain a decent steak in Israel she wasn't certain. "Perhaps the Christian cows are fatter?" she suggested.

After a while she went away to telephone again. She came back glum. No Dov. "His wife is getting suspicious that I call so often. She will be worried I am pregnant."

—

She rested her chin on a palm and stared at her empty glass. We had done in two bottles plus the beers at the King David. Through the evening, she had more than held her own. When the wine was fresh in her belly, her mood rose. When it died, her mood died, too. She mumbled something.

"What?"

"It does not matter anyway," she said. Or something close to that. Most of the syllables were in the right place.

"What doesn't matter?"

"I will never see Brickman again." Focusing on the glass, her brown eyes were slightly crossed. "The army will find him in a wadi."

"You don't know that," I said.

"Of course I do."

"If they wanted to kill him, they would have done it on the spot, both of us."

"Perhaps you they did not want to kill," she said, with significance.

"They could have shot Harry and left me standing. I was in no position to argue."

"You had Brickman's Uzi."

"No, Brickman had Brickman's Uzi, and with three guns pointed at him, he decided not to use it."

With two fingers, she pushed her empty glass until it toppled. A crescent broke off the rim and rocked back and forth, balancing a red drop. She said solemnly, "I do not believe it happened the way you say."

"How do you think it happened?"

"They were waiting for Brickman. Someone told them."

"Who would have done that?"

"You."

I tried to keep it simple. "I liked Harry."

"You are a greedy bastard. He told me." She smiled.

"Brickman was greedy, too. I will miss him. He was very nice."

He had a wife, you know, I thought—almost said it but didn't. Both of us were talking in the past tense. Anyway, he may indeed have been very nice. "Would you like some coffee?" I asked.

"Why not."

"Have you been with Agritech for long?"

She nodded, barely. The elegant nose tilted down, didn't rise again. She looked at me across the table. She had drunk more than I had, and I had drunk a lot. I thought she was going to be sick. She swallowed rapidly. After a moment she took a deep breath. "Dov hired me as his first full-time employee. He is not an administrator. He needed someone experienced."

"And you had worked as an administrator?"

"No. But I had studied this at Hebrew University. This is my first job, not counting summers on my sister's kibbutz. And it looks like it's going to . . ."

"Harry's partners may come through," I said.

"Not after Brickman is found in a wadi."

"Drink your coffee." The prim waitress had brought the check. "I'll find you a taxi. Tomorrow I'll tell Dov everything that happened."

"You can tell me, now. I want to know what happened to Brickman."

"You've heard most of it. And you wouldn't remember anything I added tonight."

"I would. You could buy us another bottle and tell me again."

"You'd start telling me I had Harry bushwhacked."

She folded her hands across her mouth. She shook her

head, and the long rope of hair thrashed the flowers behind her.

I paid the check and walked her down the driveway to King David Street. Cars streamed in both directions, yellow headlights flashing. Miss Sennesh was humming softly when I put her in a taxi.

It was 10:30 in Jerusalem, 3:30 in the afternoon in New York. I held my head under the faucet, came out with the room more or less steady. I didn't want to call Meg, but Timmy Upham or Isaiah Stern might tell me how the market was doing without Max finding out. I picked up the receiver.

There was a knock at the door. I set down the phone. So far I'd met masked gunmen, soldiers, and a dipso young woman while ducking calls from the embassy and the Yamam. If I didn't open the door, no one would get another chance to bother me.

The knock came again, insistent. A cop's knock, I thought, and opened the door.

Miss Sennesh stepped into the doorway. She raised a bottle. "They opened it for me at the bar." She kicked off her shoes, stalked into the bathroom, and came out with the bottle and two glasses in her arms. She sat heavily on the bed, and the glasses rolled in different directions. She grabbed one, poured it full, and sank back.

When I took the bottle away, she rested the glass in the V of her blouse. A little spilled every time she breathed.

There was a desk with a big fruit basket beside the windows. I sat over there.

"The reason I wish to know about Brickman," she said

with too perfect and painfully steady diction, "is that he was important to our business. Did the Arabs hurt him?"

"One whack with a rifle." If she wanted to know, I would tell her. "They didn't keep at it."

"Was he hurt?"

"Dazed, a little. He stopped making wisecracks."

"I cannot hear you. Sit here."

I sat on the edge of the bed, watched the glass full of wine tremble.

"Was he hurt?" she said.

"I would say it hurt."

"Oh. . . ." Her confidence was fading. "Did he . . . did Brickman say anything?"

"Before they hit him, he said something like we're Americans, you assholes."

"Was he frightened?"

"I don't know."

"I do not think he would be very brave." She tried to sit up, did so with a certain amount of damage. "I never cry over things that happen." She dabbed at her shirt. "You could help me out of this." She waved with the glass, making it less a request than a directive.

I unbuttoned the blouse, pulled the tails free. Her lacy black bra hooked in front. I left it alone.

She set the wine on the nightstand, tottered into the bathroom, ran water, and came back with the shirt looking tie-dyed. She struggled into it, misaligned the buttons, and tried again. She gave me a mildly cross-eyed, businesslike stare. "I will see you at seven in the morning. Then you can tell Dov Levy what happens to our company."

"I'm sorry about Harry," I said. "He may still be alive."

"Thank you. I do not think so."

"I'll walk you down to a cab." And make sure you stay in it, I thought.

"That is not necessary." She looked at herself in the mirror, either accepted the blotches with equanimity or was too fuzzy-eyed to notice them.

I walked her down anyway, caught a sly look from the doorman. There were cabs waiting.

"Seven A.M.," she reminded me.

"What's you name, your first name?"

"Esther," she said thickly, "after the Persian queen."

SIX

Agritech's office was open early, and a burly young man with shaggy hair was communicating by computer with his employees in Ethiopia. Esther Sennesh introduced me to Dov Levy, the founder and guiding spirit of Agritech Consultants. He and his office both looked in need of an administrator. Dov Levy was a jumble of rumpled clothing, tousled hair, drooping shirttail, sagging belly. His face looked oddly disorganized as well, heavily fleshed and dark, lower lip pendulous, pouchy cheeks haphazardly dented, eyes questioning as if he'd misplaced something. Esther had told me Levy had served in the army in Lebanon and showed the wear. "Something blew up in his face," she said. "He looks much better than he did ten years ago. Not many people can say that."

The office was almost as bad. Nobody had set off a bomb, but apart from the absence of burn and blast evidence—the computers weren't smoking, and the ceiling was in place—the disorder couldn't have been much worse at ground zero. Computer printouts were scattered like antimacassars over every surface. An overturned coffee cup had spilled brown scum over a stack of file folders. Document boxes were on their sides, contents fanning across the floor. If not a bomb site, the scene could have been the handiwork of burglars. Dov Levy showed none of the consternation of a man whose office had been burglarized, and so I knew he was in his usual work environment.

Esther didn't take it so well. Looking around in dismay, she cried, "What happened after I left?"

"Weizman needed the minerals protocol. I couldn't find it."

She sighed. "I will look later. This is McCarry. He is Brickman's friend."

Levy held out a large hand. "Welcome to our humble abode. We have three contracts we cannot bid on for lack of capital. I need to hire another agronomist, another water engineer—"

"Dov!" she said. "Brickman is *missing!* He may be dead."

"Yes, yes, it does not look good." He glanced back at a computer, where a message was appearing in strings of a half dozen words at a time. Trying to guess his age, I decided he was younger than his battered appearance suggested, perhaps in his early thirties. He said to me, "The soldiers said you were ambushed coming round a curving part of road?"

"That's right."

"It's too bad an army jeep didn't surprise them."

"The guerrillas were well armed," I said. "Your soldiers might have gotten killed."

"It is possible," he said, as if he didn't believe it.

"Wouldn't they have been worried about soldiers?" Esther said. "Suppose the army *had* been coming along the highway."

"In that case, whomever the terrorists posted a mile

64

down the road on either side would have alerted the leaders, and the ambush would have faded back into the wadi." He waved a hand dismissively, implying either that he had seen his share of ambushes or that he had arranged a few. "It is not complicated. Did you see any loiterers by the road? Say a harmless-looking Bedouin gentleman leading his camel?"

"Just some kids selling sodas," I said.

"How close?"

"About a mile, I guess."

"Then you can assume they radioed ahead to tell their masters to be prepared."

I shook my head. "They were pretty friendly when I walked back. Their uncle let me call for help."

He spread his hands. "I'm certain they were friendly. But if the PLO or Hamas or another gang left them a radio and told them to use it if a certain car passes, they would do so if they wished to remain living."

"Has anybody demanded money?" Esther asked.

"Not from us. I will try to reach Brickman's partners this afternoon." The computer had finished. He bent, read the message, typed at lightning speed what I took to be a response. He finished and smiled. "From Jerusalem to Addis Ababa in half a second. If they wish to argue further with me, we shall know in a moment."

The screen remained empty.

"So, what do you remember?" he asked.

I went through the morning, from Harry's meeting me at the hotel to my walk down the highway to the Arab village. Nothing changed his mind that there had been accomplices to the gunmen posted along the highway.

"Whether they were waiting for Brickman, in particular, or just any non-army car is the only question," he said. "I don't suppose the soldiers offered speculations?"

I shook my head.

"Yamam called McCarry yesterday," Esther said.

"Really? What do they think?"

"I don't know," I said. "I didn't call them back."

He looked at me the way a scientist might who has discovered a new species of tree snail. Puzzled that it exists at all. Like, I thought, Charlie Kimball contemplating a stockbroker.

"If you were an Israeli citizen, you would not have that luxury," he said. His tone left it to me whether Israelis were unfairly put upon or foreigners got away with murder.

"If I were an Israeli citizen, I would need a new surname."

He shrugged. "Donald Ben Carry has a ring to it." He thought of something. "Did Brickman leave a blue-bound notebook with you?"

"No."

"Did he have it with him?"

"Not that I noticed."

"Ah! At least the terrorists do not have it."

"No—just Harry."

He didn't look particularly censured. Investors aren't as fungible as shekels, but in Dov Levy's book they weren't up there with blue-bound notebooks.

"It is very important to Agritech," Esther said, looking crossly at me. "Dov prepared a financial plan for the next two years just for Brickman. It's in longhand, not even on the computer. And Brickman was making notations. So if it is lost—"

"It is not a disaster," Levy said. "Just two or three weeks' work gone."

"It's probably at Brickman's house," Esther said.

"He seemed to have a lot of papers there," I agreed.

Dov Levy nodded, started to say something when a door

66

from the hall opened. A man as thick as Levy but a quarter again as tall staggered in. His arms were wrapped around a carton brimming with loose instruments. He found a flat surface two steps past the door—at his feet—and dropped the box. He flexed his thick arms, wiped a palm across his tall forehead. He was black-haired, heavily bearded, and in a sour-looking mood.

Dov Levy snapped something at him in Hebrew.

The man kicked the carton, sagged into a chair. He glowered at the smaller man.

"This is what they send us in immigrant labor," Levy said to Esther and me. "The idiot is supposed to be a computer programmer, but he cannot lift more than one box a day." If there was a non sequitur in that, he didn't notice.

"Yura is from Moscow," Esther said.

"They're all from Moscow, and they're all computer programmers. Except the ones who are engineers and surgeons. If they are from Moscow, why do their shoes smell of cow dung?"

"There must be cows in Moscow," she said, and began laughing.

"There are certainly no computer programmers in Moscow," he said. He dug around in a desk, tossed Miss Sennesh a ring of keys. "If we hope to get anything from Brickman's partners, I need that notebook. Could you check at his place? Take my car. You can drop Donald Ben Carry at his hotel."

"You're not going to try to sell me a piece of Agritech?" I said.

"I will if you wish. Despite your new surname, I do not think I would be successful."

Esther swung the keys. *"Poka,* Yura."

Yura nodded wearily.

We went down to the street. Agritech Consultants wasn't

spending lavishly on office space. The suite was above a hot dogs and sauerkraut emporium on a narrow pedestrian mall filled with fast-food shops and souvenir stores. On the way over, Esther Sennesh hadn't known what to talk about and so had talked about the New Town. The street where Agritech had its office was named Ben Yehuda, after Eliezer Ben Yehuda. "He resurrected Hebrew," she said. "It had been the language of prayer. But Ben Yehuda made it the daily language of Jews in Israel."

"Sort of like Americans picking up Chaucer's English?" I said.

"You don't understand. Coming from so many lands, they needed a common language. Now what you might say is, 'Why not an easy language?' "

I didn't, but it was a point.

She looked around, spotted a square white Fiesta wedged in next to a rack of bicycles at the end of the block. "Do you want me to drop you at the hotel?" she said.

"Are you going out to Harry's?"

"Yes. Dov needs those papers."

If Dov Levy had any more papers, Agritech would come to a standstill. But there was no point in arguing with dedication.

"I'll come with you," I said.

She opened the Fiesta's trunk, removed a battered but serviceable-looking gun. She handed it to me. "You push this, then pull that—but not until we're out of town."

"And then any camel is fair game?"

"No. Any Arab is fair game. Any *hostile* Arab," she corrected herself quickly, but I thought her preference was the first version.

*   *   *

When *we ran* into Arabs, they were the same two boys at the same soft drink stand, and Esther Sennesh threw me a quick nervous look. "You don't shoot them, all right?"

"All right." Her sense of humor was so undeveloped I couldn't risk debating the order.

We reached Shomrim Tsion without ambushes. The men on guard duty included the large, red-bearded fellow from yesterday. When Esther stopped the car, he greeted her with a huge grin and a burst of Hebrew. She responded, and both their moods became subdued. I guessed Harry was the topic.

So he had brought her here. Or she had brought herself. Either way, often enough that she knew some of the guards.

We drove up to the house. She got out, said I could leave the gun on the floor. She hurried up the path. The long, low building reflected the sun. She tried the door, which was unlocked, and went inside. When I followed, she complained, "Oh, the army leaves such a mess."

Harry Brickman hadn't had enough possessions in the place for anyone to leave much of a mess. As I stepped into the living room beside her, I decided it all depended on how you went about making the mess. If you turned over the few pieces of furniture, smashed the couple of ceramic lamps, gutted the few pillows, emptied the closets of clothing, shredded the mattress, demolished the bed platform, scattered the stacks of newspapers, and dismantled some kitchen appliances—if you did it that way, you could make a satisfactory mess.

"Why would they have done all this?" she cried. "You didn't tell me."

"They didn't do it while I was here."

Arik and some of his men had stayed behind. But they hadn't seemed interested in further searching.

69

So why had they stayed behind?

"We'll never find Dov's notebook!"

She had gone room to room, her face hiding whatever she felt. I could guess what that might be. Her gaze lingered here and there. The sight of the gutted mattress and dismantled platform held her motionless.

I grabbed a corner of broken composition board, tilted it against a wall, and stepped over to the closet. Nothing remained as I had seen it except the tennis racket on the floor. A striped business shirt was off its hanger in the corner. I reached in, yanked on a sleeve. Underneath was only bare floor. The house was too new to have dust bunnies.

"What would they have been looking for?" I said.

She came over, not answering, glanced up for permission, and leaned against me. "I know Brickman is dead."

There was no reason why a torn-up house made his death more likely, let alone certain, but I felt it, too. The spirit of the living protects their possessions. Probably untrue, but emotionally convincing.

"I want to leave," she said.

We went out to the car. The morning had started hot and was really stoking up. She sat in the driver's seat with the door open, facing ahead at nothing in particular. The house wasn't that ugly. It had shutters on the whitewashed walls, roof tiles of deeper red than the surrounding hills. If you drove up in the evening, and the settlement's lights were on, and a night of wine drinking and lovemaking beckoned, Harry's villa might be an inviting place.

I went back inside. Newspapers had been tossed about everywhere. Fragments of furniture lay atop clots of pillow stuffing. It was chaotic, but there really wasn't all that much rubble. For ten minutes I searched diligently—and then I gave it another five, looking in places I'd already looked. By the end of the second round, I was certain that none of Harry's paperwork remained. The stack had been spilling off a small table in the front room. The table lay with its legs in the air, an odd creature either inviting a mate or playing dead. Pages of the *Jerusalem Post* were scattered all over. But the documents Harry had been working on, including Dov Levy's notebook, were gone.

I went out. Down the hillside, a few of Shomrim Tsion's settlers were outdoors, spading a hole, parging a foundation, the men wearing dark hats, the women covering their heads modestly with kerchiefs. A religious community, Arik had said. There had been incidents.

After I'd left, the soldiers had torn the place apart. Either to find out whether the American had anything to do with stirring up the settlers. Or to send a message the way armies send messages, by brutal example. They couldn't blow up the house of a Jew, even a pain-in-the-ass American who ridiculed border guards. But they could tell him and his neighbors what they thought.

The image of Arik and his cadre getting a little back fitted my prejudices. But it didn't explain the absence of Harry's business papers.

When *we got* back to the hotel, there were messages from the car rental agency, the police, and the embassy. I let the operator give me the telephone numbers, wrote them down, and went for a swim, vaguely missing Esther Sennesh's gloomy company. While I was bobbing in the deep end, thinking four laps had earned me two beers, the cop came around. He was young and good-looking, with deep olive skin, hard amber eyes, a stiletto nose, and tight unromantic lips. His hair was black and straight, thinning a bit and combed neatly and precisely sideways along the tall dome of his forehead. "I am Superintendent Alboker," he announced. "Come out of the pool."

I stayed where I was. The message from the police had been from Superintendent Alboker. I looked him over. He was tall—though that may have been from my pool-level perspective—and he wore an open-necked white shirt, tan slacks, tasseled loafers. His arms were thin and hairy, his brow heavy, his eyes unused to being ignored. He held a thin leather portfolio that he tapped impatiently against his leg.

"I left two messages, which you did not return," he said. "Why did you not call back?"

"I already talked to the army."

"We are not the army. We are the National Police."

"I assumed the National Police talked to the army. But I forgot to wonder whether the army talks to the police."

"You are a guest in this country," he said, "and a small amount of respect would be in order. Come out of the pool. We must talk."

My generations-old antipathy to the police tried to rouse itself. It was fellows like this, in black and tan, who suppressed Grandfather McCarry's yearning to fall asleep one night as a drunken *free* Irishman. Or perhaps I had it confused. He might just have wanted to be an Irishman who had drunk free. Or been allowed to run a tab. In much of the McCarry family, that was as close as we came to political aspirations.

I climbed out of the pool, wrapped a towel around my neck, admired the official-looking identification he showed me, and led the way to a couple of small metal tables near the snack bar. "What's on your mind, Superintendent?"

"Tell me about the abduction of Mr. Brickman."

Some tales I would happily tell every half hour: how McCarry sent the IRS packing by finding the crucial receipt; how McCarry spat in the boss's eye; how the day after McCarry bought Wonky Toys at five, the takeover offer came at ten. For other tales, twice was too much, three times a burden. More tellings than that invited self-examination into how one could have done better. Harry's Uzi had nestled between the seats throughout the hijacking. If I'd had more courage, and had known how to fire the damned thing. . . . In all likelihood, in that case Harry and I would both be dead.

"I need a beer," I said.

"If it will loosen your tongue, be my guest." He didn't mean it literally. I bought my own, told him everything I remembered about yesterday morning. He wanted to know why Harry and I were in Israel, so I told him that. He wanted to know if Brickman was having business difficulties. I said I hadn't a clue but didn't think so.

"What about enemies?"

One corner of my mind wondered whether they asked these questions every time terrorists bushwhacked an out-of-towner. Another corner worked on the last question, which wasn't so easy.

"He invests other people's money," I said. "In that business, you get enemies."

"The clients become unhappy?"

"That, too, I guess. What I meant was, it's a competitive business. Every dollar in Harry's hands is a buck someone else can't milk. Some people resent that." I finished the Gold Star, set the bottle on the table, and shifted my feet from the flagstones to the grass, which was cooler. "You're asking odd questions about a West Bank abduction."

He didn't warm to somebody else usurping the interrogator's role. He said, "There are certain things about this abduction that are unusual. We must explore every possibility. You do not resent Mr. Brickman?"

"Only his money," I said, which wasn't true. I half resented his getting into Esther Sennesh's dungarees. It took a jerk to make a twenty-some-year-old weepy. There was no point in distracting him with that.

"You resented his money."

I sighed. "That's right. So I hit him in the head a few miles from Shomrim Tsion and made the rest up. Now you can clear your case and tell the U.S. one of its own citizens is responsible instead of some of your Arabs."

"This is no joking matter."

"What things are unusual about the abduction?"

"You are not helpful, that is unusual."

"I haven't noticed anyone looking hard for Harry. When they do, I'll be helpful."

"It would do no good—no good for your friend—to force the terrorists to kill him, if they haven't."

"Do you think they have?"

"As a policeman, I find it better to wait for facts than to speculate."

"I was asking for your professional estimate."

"These things seldom have a happy outcome." He folded one thin hand inside the other, and the knuckles on the exposed hand whitened. Nothing showed on his long face, and his voice was impersonal. "It is never good to delude the family or friends."

"Where do you think they went after leaving me?"

"You said they went north."

"What lies north?"

"Shomrim Tsion, of course. The next considerable town is Yeriho—you would say Jericho. Then more Arab towns. Aujn et Thata, El Fasayil. They could connect to Nablus. We have intelligence. Depending upon whom the abductors are, they could find refuge almost anywhere in the Territories. But it would not be safe for them for long."

"What about in Jordan? The border is so close—"

"I do not think so. A vehicle with four or five men would not get across unless we permitted it. If you wish to know, I will explain. The army had the roads closed, or at a minimum under observation, within forty minutes of your friend's capture. In that time, the abductors could not have gotten out of the Territories. But there are several highways going north and south in that part of Samaria. Side roads lead into the hills. If this was a well-planned operation, they would have had less-conspicuous vehicles waiting in a friendly place, and they would have transferred Mr. Brickman and split up. The army could not inspect the trunk of every automobile between here and Nablus."

"You're saying they couldn't have gotten him out of the country?" I'd looked at my Baedeker map. Jordan had the longest border, running almost the length of the country on the east. But Lebanon and Syria joined Israel on the north, and to the southwest, Egypt owned the Sinai.

Alboker shook his head. "They are still in Israel. Of that much, I am certain."

The stopper was in the bottle, he meant. Convenient for the police, if you could do that.

He opened the little portfolio. "I would like to show you some pictures. Tell me if you have seen this man." The photo was contrasty and showed a dark-skinned, mustached man with round cheeks grinning into the sun.

I shook my head. "Who is he?"

He debated answering. "His name is Fouad Habib. He is a terrorist who we believe has infiltrated from Lebanon."

So not all the borders were leak-proof. "A member of Hamas?"

75

"No. He is Christian. He heads a small operational unit of Fatah."

"The men who took Harry wore ski masks. If Habib was one of them, I wouldn't recognize him."

"No, of course." He got up to go. "If I call you again, please call me back. Your friend's life may hang in the balance. If there is a ransom demand, you must contact me at once. The people at my office can reach me at any time."

I *walked him* through the lobby, to where a car waited, shook his hand, and promised I would call. Then I leaned against the passenger's door. "Was it the police or the army that trashed Harry's house?"

"What are you talking about?"

"His villa was torn apart."

"When was this?"

"Sometime after the army sent me home yesterday." I explained about Agritech's financial plan and my trip with Esther Sennesh.

If he was annoyed at our own search, he didn't let on. "Thank you for the information. Yamam and the army searched but did no damage. Do you think I will find Sennesh at her office?"

"I expect so," I said.

He went off and I went back into the lobby. In a policeman's presence, I had been immune from the house rules. With the policeman gone, a small, uniformed woman rushed up and told me with a heavy Slavic accent, "Guests are not permitted in swimming attire."

"All right," I said. I headed back down to the pool.

SEVEN

The only bad part about being out of touch with the office is that the stock market picks exactly those times to throw a fit. The further you are from New York's time zone, the more spectacular the turmoil. At five P.M. Jerusalem time, I was in my room, windows open to the traffic fumes, listening to Meg Sorkin report on the Dow Jones averages' first thirty minutes. The industrial stocks were down by eighty-four points on heavy selling. The Labor Department had given out employment figures nobody liked. She didn't say whether the numbers were strong or weak, and I didn't ask. Strong meant the economy was perking up and interest rates would be going up—reason to sell stocks. Weak meant the recession was lingering and corporate profits would fall—also a reason to sell. If you wanted to sell, there was always a reason to be found.

"What do you want to do, Donald?" she said.

"How is Viscount Industries?"

She tapped the symbol and reported, "It's up an eighth."

"Okay," I said.

"Okay? Have you decided? A couple of clients have called and said they're worried. Mrs. Folger in particular."

Mrs. Folger called every week fearing a financial earthquake. I kept her in the stock market by telling her that alternative investments such as real estate were at risk of rent control or confiscation.

"If she calls again, tell her the employment numbers don't matter—nobody in government can count that high." She would like that. Mrs. Folger sent me little tracts printed in brown on gold warning about bureaucrats robbing America of its liberty. I thought she belonged to the Gordon Kahl YAF chapter.

"And *don't* tell her I'm in Israel," I said.

"I wouldn't dream of it," Meg said. She knew that Mrs. Folger suspected that Jews had a guiding hand in arranging the coming tyranny. "So what do you want to do in the accounts?"

"Nothing. Leave everything alone." I got off the phone, hoping I was right. You could never tell when a morning selling squall, born of some idiocy like a government report, would turn into something really nasty. Bad news comes hidden in gibberish. Someone had said that.

Seven hours away from the stock market, I couldn't get a feel for what was going on. Meg had read me all the relevant details about the number of stocks advancing versus those declining, the up-versus-down volume, and more arcane items like TICK and TRIN measures of the market's direction. But none of those figures replaced the intuitions earned by sitting in front of a quotation machine for hours and watching the electronic ticker report each trade.

People whose intuitions are top-notch can make a fine living trading the market hour by hour. I'm not that good, but I like to have the screen close.

I wondered if brainy young Howie Harslip, our chairman's recruit, was using my quote screen right now. Meg hadn't said whether he'd moved into my office.

I went downstairs.

The television actor and his entourage staggered into the lobby, sunburned and scuffed. A couple wore T-shirts saying MASADA. I remembered Harry telling me about the mountaintop stronghold. A monument to Jewish obstinacy, he'd said. The actor tried to gather his troops around him. He had something to say, and he wanted to say it in the middle of the lobby of the King David Hotel. But people kept drifting off, desperate for a shower or a drink or not to hear the fellow's pronouncement. After a minute, he decided he didn't have a quorum and limped off, chin high, trailed by a well-packaged blonde and the large white-haired woman who seemed to be directing things. The trip up Masada had left the blonde wilted, but the older woman looked like she hadn't broken a sweat.

A tall young man with pale hair and a bulging Adam's apple swept in, the tails of his tan suit flapping applause. He stopped at the desk and asked a clerk in the pinched tone of a Boston grandee: "Donald McCarry's suite, please."

She gave him the room number. So much for guests' privacy. But then, Superintendent Alboker had tracked me down at the pool pretty easily.

I followed, then passed him by as he waited for the elevator. He wasn't all that young, I saw, getting a closer look at the bony face, mid-thirties at least, which wasn't young at all if you were an errand boy from the embassy chasing down Americans who didn't return phone calls.

The stairs were a few yards past the bar. I sprinted up three floors and was forty feet down the hall and mostly out of sight when he got off the elevator.

79

He found my door, rapped lightly, put his hands in his pockets, tapped his toe to tell the world he was impatient.

I leaned against the wall. I could sit here, in one of the well-worn Regency chairs, and admire the pretty flower arrangements with which the King David decorated its staircase, or I could go down the hall and get taken over the jumps one more time by somebody who thought Harry's kidnapping was his business. If it would help recover Harry, I would talk to embassy munchkins all day long. But I didn't think the embassy would be the ones to spring Harry. So I settled back and stared at the opposite wall, and he tapped on the door again—a gentle, noninsistent summons—and I explained to myself that a distaste for officialdom was an inherited quirk, just like a bald spot or an overbite. Jack McCarry—"Jackie" to his friends, most of whom knew officialdom from its habit of interrupting their dice games—espoused a number of principles from which he never wavered. One of them was never talk to a cop unless you knew you could beat the rap. He talked too often, bet too often he could beat their best rap, and spent too many of his years regretting his impulsiveness. I'd picked up his wariness of officialdom at the Sunday supper table, on the occasions when he wasn't doing time or chasing someone else's woman. How much else of Jackie McCarry I'd inherited I wasn't sure. Only a man with a larcenous heart becomes a stockbroker, said a friend who knew both McCarry generations. He at least half-approved. He'd have approved, too, of my sitting tight while the embassy messenger went about his business. Cops, prosecutors, stock market regulators, army captains, more cops and embassy lackies—they were all part of the mass of officially employed humanity that I distrusted.

A final *tap tap tap*. The little woodpecker from the embassy hoping I was home but not wanting to disturb any afternoon naps if I wasn't.

I looked around the corner in time to see his right leg disappear into my room, following the rest of him that was already out of sight.

That sat me up straight.

Either someone had let him in or he'd jimmied the door. He'd given himself plenty of time with his patient little taps.

I got up and went down the hall softly, without a thought of alerting hotel security. They probably granted the embassy ransacking rights anyway, as long as the blond Brahmins only burglarized their own countrymen. Bringing hotel security into the picture would embarrass the idiot, show him up as a careless workman. He would turn pink and sputter. I didn't want to share that sight.

The decision to feed him part of the carpet came only between the time I knocked, calling "Room service!" and the first movement of the door. Then I put my shoulder into it, the door swung wide, and my visitor's mouth dropped. "Afternoon," I said, and lobbed a punch at his nose—easing up at the last instant because a voice said *How do you know he's not from Avis? You've been dodging them, too*—and easing up saved me from getting hurt. He grabbed my wrist in midflight without trying, pulled it in a way that swung me against the wall about the time a knee hammered my abdomen twice. Still holding my wrist, he pitched me into the center of the room.

I hit the carpet without bouncing.

Also without breathing for a moment. My innards had been hammered by a steam shovel. If I was lucky, the shovel would excavate the damaged parts on its next pass.

I finally managed to do more than just lie there. I worked up a loud, gurgling gasp.

The grandee was a few feet away, going about his business, which consisted of going through my things. He had his back partly to me. He didn't seem concerned I might get a second wind, find a wheelchair, and roll up for a second round. I didn't blame him. After a minute of watching him sort through my clients' portfolios, I got an elbow under me. A minute later, when he had given up on the stocks and bonds and was rummaging through a stack of annual reports that I'd read on the plane, I sat up.

"You're pretty stupid," he said over his shoulder.

I looked around for something to hit him with. A brass lamp would do fine. The lamps were small ceramic onions and in any case out of reach.

"I could have killed you," he went on. He sounded less like the famous Bostonians I knew than like David Frye imitating them. A little JFK, a little Bugs Bunny, a tenor voice halfway between a creaking floorboard and a Boston bean fart.

"*You're* the one caught black bagging a room," I said.

He looked around. Long face, lots of bones, deeply sunk eyes, jaw and teeth from Mother's side of the family, if she'd been bred in a stable. He gave me a lot of the teeth in a grin that looked almost friendly. "That's your version."

"Who are you?"

"Spaulding. Sorry about the knee. Fortunately, at the last moment I realized you weren't a threat."

He wasn't rubbing it in. I got halfway up, slid onto the bed. My lunch was staying down. The steamshovel had left an ache that reached from breastbone to crotch. Not bad for two bumps. I got onto my feet, reached the bathroom, ran water and splashed my face. My hands were trembling.

Tough guy, McCarry. Used to the stock market's subtler violence.

I dried my face, wobbled out. "What can I do for you, Spaulding?"

"We-ll . . ." The board creaked. "Probably not much. Why didn't you get back to us? Brickman was your friend. The United States Embassy can help in situations like this."

"Help whom, the next of kin?"

"If it works out that way."

"Are you done looking through my shirts?"

He tossed a Brooks Brothers back, fingered a Viscount Industries annual report. "You're not a broad reader. Personally, I spend every hour I can with Henry James."

"He must not have any choice. Do you have any news on Harry?"

"No. What were you two doing?"

"Harry lives here part of the time. He was pitching an investment to me, hoping I'd pitch it to my clients."

"What sort of investment?"

He was waiting for the answer with an open half-grin. He already knew, I thought, which was curious.

"Agritech Consultants Limited. It's an Israeli company," I said. "Maybe you've heard of them?"

"I don't invest much. What's your friend's interest in an Israeli company?"

"He owns part of it, with his partners and a few clients."

"That doesn't answer my question."

"He's a late-blooming Zionist, a believer."

"Yeah—a lot of people living in the United States would put Israel first, if it came to it. You know the ones I mean." He scanned the room, spotted nothing that assigned me to the fifth column or didn't.

"You could always bring back loyalty oaths," I suggested, but he hadn't come by to notice insults.

"What's your understanding of what Agritech does?" he said, except it came out like Bugs asking Elmer.

"Crop development in the Third World."

"Would you say it's a lucrative business?"

"Not so far. You put money up today and hope money comes back in two years." I thought a moment and added, "Your customers aren't the best credit risks."

"But Harry Brickman's high on it?"

"Believers have blind spots."

He gave that open-mouthed smile. "You never notice the warts on your true love's ass. How much have Brickman and his friends invested in Agritech?"

A couple of million, I guessed. The big bucks were supposed to come in this financing round, to hire more agronomists, water engineers, and bid writers. As I watched Spaulding, of the quick key set, stir my underwear, I said, "I don't know. Did you find anything at Brickman's villa?"

"Piss poor timing for me. I was up near Haifa yesterday. By the time I got down there, Brickman's place was torn apart. A neighbor said the army came back in the afternoon. They don't seem to like each other, the neighbors and the army." When that bit of chattiness evoked no reciprocal outpouring from me, he gave up on my clothes, tucked his long hands into his pockets. "The embassy doesn't employ me to give investment advice to tourists, but it's my personal opinion you're out of your mind to risk money in this country. If they didn't live at the U.S.'s tit, the place would collapse. That might not be a bad thing."

I said, "What's your guess on Brickman?"

"I'd guess they whacked him and didn't want the body discovered right away. The question I keep stumbling on is

84

why. Why Brickman? New York Jews pour into this place by the thousands. Why go after this one?"

"Why do you think?"

"Could be coincidence," he said, taking his hands from his pockets and straightening his tie. He couldn't have gotten rumpled roughing me up. He gave me a card that said Keith Spaulding, *Second Secretary*, and headed for the door saying, "Call me."

"What were you hoping to find at Harry's—or here?"

"Something to tell me why he was taken." He paused at the door. "When the army interrogated you, did you get a feeling about who they think did it?"

"I got an impression the captain didn't think it was the PLO, despite the green T-shirts. From what I saw of the border guard, I could believe someone popped over from Jordan and drove back with Harry, but a local cop says it's not likely."

"Which cop did you talk to?"

"Superintendent Alboker."

Spaulding nodded. "He's right, but 'impossible' would be a better word. One or two men get across on foot every now and then, and the Israelis kill them. Every time. It's policy. A while back, a soldier was court-martialed after three terrorists came across up in Ha Galil. They didn't do any damage because the soldiers killed two of them right off, but the third escaped back across the border into Jordan, and that embarrassed the army."

"So border crossings aren't impossible."

"Impossible without the Israelis catching on, or just about. They've got a very effective system. If Tzachi Alboker doesn't think anybody crossed, they didn't; at least not on wheels. Probably not on foot. Those army jeeps you saw—they patrol the green line every day. They drag big barbed wire rolls that rake the soil. Then they come back

85

along the same ground, hour after hour, with a Bedouin tracker sitting in back looking at the ground. If a stone's been disturbed, the Bedouin spots it. The Israelis claim they can tell if a yellow scorpion has walked across. They kill a lot of scorpions."

"I see."

"That leaves Alboker and the army looking at their homegrown crowd then: terrorists or freedom fighters, depending on your vantage. Or," he added, "the settlers at Shomrim Tsion. They're zealots, but so far they haven't gone in for kidnapping."

I *went downstairs* to the bar, figuring no one would dare put his knee in my belly if I was paying house prices for Scotch. Dov Levy and Esther Sennesh descended from opposite sides. "He was not hiding from you," Esther told her boss. He had accommodated the King David's dress code by tucking the right half of his shirt into sagging trousers.

"You know Brickman's partners," he said to me. "Do you have influence with them?"

"None at all."

His rumpled face collapsed, though the hope couldn't have been strong. He brushed a hand at a bartender who thought that to take up a stool, he should drink. "We have a problem," he said.

Any response would have invited him to explain the problem, so I took a sip of overpriced Scotch. He decided that was encouragement enough and said, "Agritech is *very* short of capital. We were counting on the additional investment by Brickman."

"That sounds like a problem," I agreed.

"I understand that without Brickman participating, you would not invest." When I didn't contradict him, he said,

"That's only reasonable, since you are not familiar with the company. But Brickman's partners are not familiar, either, and I have to approach them. I was hoping you would help me."

"How would I do that?"

"You could point out the obvious. Their firm already has invested in Agritech. If Agritech can't scrape by the next month, their investment will be a total loss."

"They might decide it's already that," I said. "If you're broke, you're broke."

"We never expected to be profitable at this stage. Brickman understood that."

"His partners may, too. If they don't, nothing I say will convince them."

Dov Levy sighed. "You are right, of course. It was wishful thinking on my part. I will phone Morgenstern and Ozick on bended knees and hope I can win a small advance, until we see how things have gone with Brickman." He slid off the stool. It was like watching a stack of laundry collapse. He spoke past me, to Miss Sennesh, who'd had nothing to say. "I'm going back to the office. You can have the car."

She nodded. He was barely out the door when she ordered a glass of wine. "Do you think they will turn him down?" she asked.

"They'll probably provide him with pocket money for a couple of weeks, until they can look things over."

"And then?"

"Agritech may be too long-range for their investing style," I said, which was as diplomatic as I could be. Agritech didn't fit any sensible person's investment style. And Morgenstern Ozick, like most aggressively run partnerships, had a time horizon of tomorrow noon.

"Dov will be sad."

"And you?"

She was already sad, but she didn't say it. "I will find another job, of course. It will not be difficult now that I am an experienced administrator."

A page cruised through the bar, announcing, "A call for Mr. McCarry." He accented the first syllable, the way they do with their pricier beer Maccabee, and I ignored him.

An elbow dug my ribs. "It might be about Brickman," Esther said.

It might indeed. Everything under the sun was about Brickman.

She signaled the barman, who brought a phone. She lifted the receiver, handed it to me, and a voice said breathlessly: "Is there any news?"

I didn't recognize the voice. It was a strong baritone, insistent, expecting to be recognized. I said, "Who is this?"

"This is Warren Morgenstern." He managed to bring a hammer down on every other syllable. "Is there news?"

I sipped my Scotch. It was almost seven P.M. in Jerusalem, midday in New York. He should be going to lunch, and I should be looking for dinner. "No news," I said, "but Dov Levy wants to talk to you."

"What about a ransom demand? We can wire money."

"No ransom demand." If he wanted to wire money, Superintendent Alboker could deal with the legalities.

"Karen's with me," he said. "She's not good."

Esther Sennesh's hand pressed my arm. She mouthed a silent "What?"

"She's holding herself together," Warren Morgenstern said.

"I'm glad to hear it. If anything breaks, I'll call you."

"Call me?" he croaked. "Call me? You should be here meeting me, meeting *us*. Didn't you get my message?"

"Where are you?"

88

"At Ben Gurion Airport, where do you think? With Karen Brickman. Do you understand? You should have brought a car. I've got six suitcases and I have to take a cab to Jerusalem?"

"It's only an hour's ride," I said, and hung up, wondering how he expected to wire money for a ransom. Assure somebody it was just another cash infusion for Agritech?

"Who was that?" Esther Sennesh said.

"A partner of Harry's."

She picked up her wine. "Damn, damn, damn."

"Why damn?"

"Americans are bossy. He will get in the way."

"He's at the airport and headed here."

"Which airport?"

"Ben Gurion. Is there another?"

"Jerusalem has an airport north of here, but small."

"There's time to finish your drink," I said.

"No. There's much I must discuss with Dov before Brickman's partner appears."

She grabbed the phone before the barman could retrieve it, but Dov hadn't had nearly enough time to get back to Ben Yehuda Street.

While she phoned and cussed, I had time to sit and wonder what Spaulding suspected Harry was up to. It was possible he lacked an idea and just got paid to be suspicious. She slammed the receiver down, and I ordered another drink.

EIGHT

When *Esther came* back from the ladies' room, I tried to calm her down by mentioning that Brickman's partner was bringing Mrs. Brickman in tow.

"The bitch," she said.

Karen Brickman turned out to be a petite brunette with a sweet, haggard smile and no sign of bitchiness. She was in her mid-thirties, mother of Little Aaron, who was staying with her brother in the Jersey suburbs. She was red-eyed and pale but was keeping herself together when we met in the hotel's bar at 10:30. She accepted Esther Sennesh as the vice president of Agritech, about which she knew only that Harry was an investor. She was confused about the time, thought it must be later in New York, and admitted she didn't travel much farther than the Atlantic beach towns. Over a Campari and soda, she started nodding and apologized just enough. "I think it's the relief," she said. Her husband hadn't been found dead, which was the fear that had kept her awake during the eleven hours from New York.

Warren Morgenstern looked relieved, too. He was about

twenty years older than Harry, thirty years older than Harry's second wife, and the years and the tension weighed on him. His face was an assemblage of pouches; the cheeks sagged in unbroken arcs from under the eyes to his jaw. The long sideburns and gray curls billowing above the ears made him look older. He wore a dark pinstriped suit, a crisp white shirt, and a maroon and gray necktie. His eyes were bloodshot, his mouth drooping.

Between them, they had wanted to know everything that had happened in the last thirty-six hours. My version played down the willingness of Harry's abductors to shoot. I could give that version to Morgenstern when we were alone. Esther listened silently as she sized up Mrs. Brickman.

"Harry always said he was lucky," Karen Brickman said.

"He *is* lucky," Morgenstern said. "He's got family and friends who care."

That was a nice epitaph, but a stock trader wouldn't say it added up to luck. Coming out ahead was lucky, though most of them insisted then it was brains.

Morgenstern's eyes turned my way. "It's important we get the message to these people that Harry is worth a lot to them unharmed."

"You'd better leave your money in New York," I said. "The Israelis won't let you pay a ransom to terrorists."

"We can see about that when the time comes." He turned to Esther. "We'll meet with Levy first thing tomorrow."

She said, "He will be ready to see you."

That was an understatement.

"And we'll talk to the police tonight."

"Warren," Karen Brickman said, "maybe we should—"

"This needs to be gotten off center." Warren Morgenstern looked at his watch. Mine said quarter to eleven. His said it was time to bother people.

Esther remembered she had Dov Levy's car and volunteered to drive them to the police headquarters. It was in Sheikh Jarrah, in East Jerusalem, she said, but there might not be anyone there to talk to them.

"That's taken care of."

I saw them off. Morgenstern had a message to deliver. The Israelis hadn't lost a cheesy little Brooklyn dentist. Brickman was a big man on Wall Street. If they fucked this one up they needn't send the immigration minister shaking his tin cup in the financial district next year. I wished him luck, hoped he didn't get himself and Mrs. Brickman thrown in jail, but didn't hope too hard.

I wondered how much of his concern was authentically for his partner, whose indispensability wasn't even hinted at with an "& Co." on Morgenstern Ozick's letterhead. He had at least as much reason to worry about his firm's capital—the small part that had been invested in Agritech—as about Harry's neck.

I went upstairs, confirmed my flight for the next day, checked in with New York for the late afternoon prices. The sell-off was about the same as it had been in the morning. That it was no worse passed for good news. When I got off the phone with Meg, the message light was on. I called downstairs.

"The concierge has a package for you, sir. Shall I send it up?"

My last evening in Jerusalem, I felt guilty about sitting in the room watching television. Deciding it was never too late to drink alone, I said, "Don't bother. I'll pick it up later."

I put on a jacket, no necktie, and walked downstairs. The terrace was busy, as were both bars. The Hollywood set were entertaining people in the watering hole to the left of the reception area, including people who didn't want to be entertained. The sign over the door said: KING DAVID'S

92

SLING SHOT BAR. On the inside it could have been a Wall Street dive, except Wall Streeters would have thrown out the singing actor.

Behind me, a voice said, "If he starts 'Hava Nagila,' I'm calling the cops." The speaker was the hefty, white-haired woman who was part of the celebrity's troupe. Her words were meant not for me but for a tall young woman who smiled and nodded as if she were used to summoning the law.

I went out the front door. A couple were getting into a taxi as the man said, "They've got belly dancing, but only Russian girls."

Hearing this, the doorman looked blankly over the couple's head. He had heavy Slavic features, grainy skin, dark eyes, and lips pursed in annoyance.

I walked down King David Street, cut across the heavy traffic and took a street running diagonally behind the YMCA. There was a Moriah Hotel sitting back behind a line of pines. It didn't have a bar, and the large open lounge had a loud party going on. I went back outside and noticed— parked nonchalantly at the curb—a white Mercedes that looked remarkably similar to the one that had been idling in the King David's driveway a few minutes earlier. I couldn't see into the passenger compartment. It had to be one of Superintendent Alboker's boys, or one of Spaulding's.

Or a poor soul looking for a hotel room.

Down Keren Hayesod, I bore right and took a twisty windy course. Twenty minutes later I found myself back at King David Street. In the interim, I hadn't spotted anything that looked like a hot nightspot. An Italian restaurant, yes, and a pizza parlour, a *glatt* kosher French restaurant, an array of hotels and official buildings, but nothing that would take my mind off other people's business for the evening.

As I walked up the driveway to my hotel, the muted yellow headlights of the Mercedes flashed through the trees behind me.

Have a long night, fellas.

I said the hell with David's Sling Shot and was on the stairway when I remembered the package the concierge was holding for me. I turned around. The trip back to the desk wasn't worth it. A clerk handed me a largish white envelope imprinted with Hebrew characters and the familiar name Avis. I squeezed the envelope and felt the give of paper. Instead of drinking the night away, or applauding Russian belly dancers, I would fill out insurance forms for Avis's shot-up car.

I took the envelope upstairs, threw it on the desk, picked out a peach from the hotel's fruit basket, and sat down to shuffle papers.

What came out of the upended package wasn't a wad of claims forms but a small journal bound in soft covers. A note was taped to the front:

This was in the car you returned.

A nice way of putting it, the car I had returned.

The pages were filled with cramped printing, in English. If this was the financial plan Dov Levy had prepared for Harry, he had gone to the trouble of translating from Hebrew. It was densely written, with hand-drawn tables and a rough box diagram. Given the obvious effort involved, it was a wonder Levy hadn't done the plan on a computer.

Glancing at the box chart, I was reminded of research reports showing how much Company A owns of Company B and, through B, of Companies C and D. There were more boxes than a litter of kittens, and each was identified by a Hebrew character.

Nothing explained what the letters stood for, and nothing described the purpose of the table. It might not be an ownership table at all but an employment table.

The text discussed competing rates of return—U.S. Treasuries, Israel bonds, LIBOR, and so on, versus AG'TECH CONS 9%—and then below veered into the political benefits of helping LDCs (I translated: less-developed countries) to raise their agricultural productivity. Leading the list was INT'L STANDING, followed by ENHANCED STABILITY. I assumed the dividend in world esteem accrued to Israel, and stability to the less-developed countries. So it was only partly a financial plan. Dov Levy also hoped to excite the reader's do-gooder impulse.

I tossed the book onto a stack of shirts I was getting ready to pack. Tomorrow I could give it to Morgenstern or drop it in the mail to Dov Levy.

I was pushing dirty socks into my bag when it occurred to me there was something odd about Levy's projections for Agritech. A *lot* might be odd, but one thing in particular stood out. The table of comparative returns showed nine-point-o percent for Agritech. Harry Brickman had told me the target was something like forty percent a year. There's nothing wrong with earning nine percent, of course. The momentum of compounding doubles money at nine percent in just over seven years. Depending on where inflation and interest rates stood, nine percent could be a respectable return on a low-risk portfolio. For partnership money, which is willing to take bigger risks for bigger returns, a target of forty percent was closer to a manager's goal. If you were good, and lucky, the actual return might be half that. That was when a money manager told his clients the truth: That over an extended period, few people would do better than twenty percent and most wouldn't do as well. You tell them that their money is doubling every three years, nine months, and three days, and if they have a glimmering of the fact that that will make them rich in a decade or so, they stay with you.

Harry would know all that, know it a lot better than I did and in infinitely finer nuance. I had enough of it right, I thought, to know he wouldn't put clients' money into something with a projected return of nine percent.

Because for aggressively managed money, nine percent was running too far behind the pack.

Because projected returns were always higher than actual returns.

Because a manager who loses his clients hasn't got a business.

He especially wouldn't settle for nine percent in a high-risk number like Agritech Consultants.

Although . . . , a skeptical inner voice whined, *he just might do it for an Israeli company. Mightn't he?*

In that case, he might. For the right Israeli company.

A guy from Jersey doesn't drive around with an Uzi within reach unless he believes strongly in something. Once the belief was there, the Uzi and the hurled rocks and the barren landscape would become badges of honor. A few million dollars, a small percentage of the pool one managed, might be let out at a lower than normal return in a good cause.

It's *other* people's money, Harry. And I could imagine his chipper response: *"Yeah, but most of them are good Jews, and if they aren't investing in Israel, they should be."*

If I'd never put my own interests ahead of a client's, I'd have muttered the word "jerk" in the silent room. He *was* a jerk. But I wasn't the one to tell him so.

Karen Brickman rang my room at quarter past twelve, full of apologies. "If you hadn't answered on the first ring, I'd have hung up," she said. "You weren't sleeping?"

"It's okay," I said. "Did the police have more to say?"

"I don't know what Warren hoped they could say. I assume they're doing their best. Official agencies usually do their best, whatever that is, don't they? There was a man with a funny name, Aloker, Alo——something, who looked as tired as I feel. He seemed very competent. So did a man from the embassy."

"Spaulding?"

"Yes, Mr. Spaulding. He didn't contribute much, but he seemed very interested."

I made uh-hums. If Alboker and Spaulding were at the meeting, neither had been tailing me around the block. Which meant nothing; each would have gofers.

She said, "They both seemed to be acting strangely. That's why I'm calling. I don't want to offend you, Mr. McCarry, but I'm too exhausted to be diplomatic. Perhaps, also, too frightened. Is there something more in this than you've told the police?"

"What sort of something?"

"Something involving you."

"No, Mrs. Brickman. Do the police think that?"

"I think it bothers them that they don't know who took Harry. Or why Harry was taken. They asked me a lot of questions about you, which I'm afraid I couldn't answer. Mr. Spaulding told Warren that you weren't cooperative."

"I told them as much as I knew," I said. My belly hadn't broken Spaulding's knee. What did he want? It was too late in the evening for me to confide in her the reasons the McCarrys didn't like cops. It wouldn't help my standing with Alboker or Spaulding, anyway.

She broke the silence, voice wavering. "Harry didn't *act* like this trip was unusual."

"Would he have told you?" It was a harsh question, but I wanted to know.

"He absolutely would have. We don't believe in keeping secrets from one another."

"That's the best way," I said.

"But you can't think of anything unusual?"

"Harry was upbeat, eager to show me his villa, eager to show me the local company. As far as I could tell, your husband felt it was just another business trip."

Somebody else had had a different view.

I *saw Warren* Morgenstern at breakfast and gave him Dov Levy's notebook. He would have to make the next decision: throw more partners' money into Agritech, or give it a decent burial. I'd turned the pages of Dov's business plan for another forty minutes after Mrs. Brickman said goodnight. If it was typical of Israeli business plans, the country had worse problems than bankrupt kibbutzes (*kibbutzim*, I corrected myself; that was what Harry called them). There was no rational development of the business laid out, no month by month projection of revenues versus costs, nothing on underlying assumptions, nothing about business risks in the Third World. Nothing, in short, that you could point to and say: "Is this reasonable (or adequate or too optimistic)? Should we assume more deadbeat customers?" Instead, the notebook was filled with technical details on agronomy that could have been lifted from a textbook, long profiles of target markets (in Ethiopia, Somalia, Tanzania, etc.) that also had a rehashed flavor. On the last page was a table entitled "Guaranteed Return to Investors" followed by a column of entries that read: "Year One: 9.0%; Year Two: 9.0%; Year Three: 9.0%" and so on down to "Year 19 & Thereafter: 9.0%."

I'd seen offerings like that before. We'd done one at Magee & Temple called Qwik-Lik Lube Shops. It was a limited partnership promising investors a minimum return of seven percent, the payments guaranteed by an insurance company. A few months later, Qwik-Lik couldn't make a payment, and the insurance company reneged on its policy.

Dov Levy hadn't put anything into Agritech's plan that told you whether you should believe the nine percent or not. The return was described as guaranteed. No mention was made of who was behind the guarantee.

Harry hadn't, as far as I could remember, mentioned any such arrangement.

"It's skimpy," I said, handing the notebook to Morgenstern. He couldn't have slept more than six hours, and his internal clock must be telling him it was just past one in the morning. But he looked ready to give a little hell to the rest of the Israeli government.

He thumbed a few pages. "A hand-written business plan? Who did such a thing?"

"Dov Levy. He was eager to get it back." I told him about the drive with Miss Sennesh out to Shomrim Tsion and how the notebook had turned up in the rental car.

"I'll read it. So far, it doesn't impress me. When do you go home?"

"This evening."

He didn't accuse me of deserting a friend. He nodded. "You have clients to attend to; I understand. Business goes on. I've left Ben Ozick in charge of everything—*everything*—hoping he will consult with me on the large decisions. God knows."

Ozick was mainly a trader.

"One cannot let others run his business for long," he said.

"I prefer to screw things up myself," I agreed. "Tell me something. Was Agritech Harry's pet or did you all agree to it?"

"Both. We all found the idea acceptable in principle.

99

Harry set the company up, Harry and Dov Levy. And Harry monitors its progress."

"Has Morgenstern Ozick invested a lot in the company?"

"We and our limited partners have put in just over three million. Not much these days, but I would not care to explain to our partners how we lost that sum."

He might have to do so. But he and Ozick could point the finger at Harry.

"What do you plan to do today?" I asked.

"First, I'm going to have a talk with the U.S. ambassador. Then a few words with the minister of police. Then I suppose I'd better have a look at Agritech Consultants."

Mrs. Brickman hadn't joined us for breakfast by the time I went back upstairs. I phoned Agritech, and Esther Sennesh answered.

"Your boss's notebook turned up," I said. "Warren Morgenstern has it."

"I will tell Dov." She used a high, martyred tone. Karen Brickman's arrival had put another woman at the center of the Harry drama—worse, a woman with a superior claim to be there. She must have read my mind, because she said, "Does she think Brickman is alive?"

"I don't know. I think she's still hopeful."

"I am not," she said solemnly. "I know he is dead."

I disregarded the possibility that she did know. "You're just depressed. This is stressful."

"That is American jargon, isn't it? An Israeli would never say stressful. Our entire lives are stressful. What is new?" When I didn't answer, she said, "When are you leaving?"

"Tonight."

"You bought me dinner, so I will buy you lunch."

"Um—"

"I want you to tell me more about Brickman—more

about his business." She added quickly, "It may help the police."

I couldn't see how that mattered, if he was dead. But I didn't want to pick the wings off her self-respect, so I said I would see her at noon.

Dov Levy wasn't at Agritech's headquarters. The big Russian gofer, whose name I'd forgotten, had the top off a computer and was scratching his head with four fingers. Esther introduced us again, chattered something at him in Hebrew which Yura gave no sign of understanding. We went into the hall, closed the door behind us, and she put her hands in her pockets. Her dark eyes were solemn, like a Persian queen's inspecting a spear carrier who might be loyal but probably was fickle. "What time is your plane?"

"Nine o'clock."

"Let's see if Dov left his car."

"We can get a taxi, have lunch at the hotel."

She shook her head. "I can't look at that woman. It's absurd. She is dreadful, so what do I care what she thinks of me?"

We went downstairs. Dov Levy's car belonged to the company, she explained. They had not wasted investors' money; the Fiesta had been bought used from Dov's father-in-law. If only it were parked nearby. She looked up and down Ben Yehuda Street and checked two side streets before giving up. "He must be interviewing," she said, shrugging. "We need another person in Ethiopia, and there are several candidates. We have to thank the immigration. Dov is right that Yura is hopeless, but many of the Russians coming in are highly qualified."

Four young men in snug-fitting black overcoats and

fedoras passed, silent and intent. All wore beards. Three wore horn-rimmed glasses. Nodding after them, Esther said, "If we had fewer rabbis and religious students, we would be better off. They don't serve in the army. They don't hold jobs. They bless things when they are paid and curse the rest. Are there religious parties in the United States?"

"Not exactly. All sides claim God votes for them."

"A friend opened a pizza restaurant, which he wanted to be kosher. So it was necessary to have a rabbi approve the kitchen and the food preparation. The rabbi does this every night, and he eats free at my friend's restaurant—not just the rabbi but also the *rebbetzin*, his brother, and three teen-aged sons, a whole table full of them. Do you mind walking for a while?"

We set off along a side street crowded with flower vendors and vegetable stands. Esther seemed oblivious to the scene and the motor scooters that wove among the pedestrians. I tried to imagine her in lower Manhattan, rushing to meet Harry after work. It almost worked. She had the snug American blue jeans, white running shoes, and a long-sleeved jersey that would blend in, and the rest of her would set the standard for the neighbors.

"We complain about everything, all the time," she said. "But before listening to Brickman, I did not look at things quite the way I do now. He says we are strangling ourselves with socialists, religious zealots, and bureaucrats. Do you think so?"

"I haven't been here long," I said.

"But it is different from the United States?"

"Not that different."

"Are the States strangling?"

Thinking of the way the stock market had broken, I didn't answer right away. You could never tell when a sick stock market was a warning that the economy was headed for trouble. If share prices fell a few hundred points, it was easy to imagine the sky coming down, too. I said, "It's harder to wreck a big economy."

"Why, if you have the same problems?"

"We don't, exactly. Even if we did, a larger economy offers more loopholes. There are more people looking for angles, working off the books, who keep things going."

"Brickman said that is called the 'black' economy."

I wondered about their bedtime chatter. "The black economy is extremely efficient: no subsidies; no set-asides; no quotas; no tax-motivated transactions—just supply and demand. You do something—paint a house, grow sweet corn—because you expect to make money and keep it."

She gripped my hand and swung it up cheerfully. "Between the two of you, I'll have a degree in economics, at least the illegal kind."

"Where are we going?"

"We'll be there soon."

"*Harry and I* came here," she said. It was Harry, not Brickman.

"To see the sights?"

"Yes, for sight-seeing."

The view was splendid. Outside the narrow tower window, the skeletal wooden frame of a windmill blade cast shadows on us. From the window I could see across a deep gorge into the twisted streets of the old walled city. Tourists and guards walked atop the battlements.

"Brickman is dead," she said, "and the skinny woman will mourn him."

"You don't know that."

She shrugged. "I know."

She unloaded the groceries we had bought along the way: a bottle of Golan Heights wine, hummus, pita, tomatoes. The windmill's manager had gone to school with her, and she had the key.

"We can have our picnic, and you can tell me more about Harry. Not about Wall Street. I don't care about that."

"I don't know much about Harry apart from what he does on Wall Street."

"You weren't friends?"

"Not really."

"You were never to his house—"

"No."

She emptied her paper cup, refilled it. She settled her back against the stone wall next to me. "He said his wife is a shrew. Do you think she is?"

"It's possible. I only met her last night."

"So it is possible. And possible Brickman was a liar."

Definitely, I thought.

Without looking, I knew her head had dipped. She had herself a quiet cry. She punched my knee, held out her cup. I knew where she was heading. We weren't holding a wake for Harry. We were saying to hell with him. When the bottle was finished, she came around in front of me on her knees, wobbling as if the building were rocking. She brushed a hand along my face, held an ear in the V of her fingers. "I think you may be a nicer man than Brickman."

If she thought she needed consoling for Brickman, the wine wasn't enough. Neither would I be.

She pushed her face into my neck, mumbled something that meant, "Is this place all right?"

"As long as your friend doesn't have a key."

"She has. We share this place. The tourists don't know."

"Tourists come here?" I was too drowsy to imagine flash-cubes popping, but thought I should feel alarmed.

Esther stretched lazily. "Shall I point out the important sights? The Mount of Olives is here," she said, touching a dark breast. "Then the Valley of Kidron, and here—here is the Lion Gate."

I explored the geography gently, and when she groaned and shuddered I thought only that Harry had been a jerk if he'd gotten himself killed. Esther nuzzled me and said, "And then you have visited the Tomb of the Virgin, long dead. . . ."

Twenty minutes later, she jabbed her fist against my ribs, waking me, and we went just as happily over the same ground.

NINE

They let me get on the plane before coming aboard. Both were large, with heavy shoulders and narrow hips, shirt tails hanging loosely over baggy gray slacks, running shoes looking just out of the box. They didn't have to ask anybody to point me out. They came from different directions, converging across a center row and shouldering down an aisle. And although they wore civilian clothes and could have been taxi drivers or baggage handlers, I didn't have to ask who they were. Security of some kind. I'd spent forty minutes with El Al security before boarding, going through their patented hundred-questions routine that began, "Ah, this was your first visit to Israel?" and came back to that one twice, interspersed with ninety-seven others designed to detect the inconsistency of a traveler up to no good. "Ah, did you enjoy your time in Israel?" Yes, thank you, except for the prevalence of cops and terrorists, it was lovely.

These two opened wallets with badges. "We would like to talk to you," said one.

"There is a private place outside," said the other. "Did you bring luggage aboard?"

He collected my bags from the overhead bins and we made our way down the aisle. Men in fedoras glanced up. Women in kerchiefs tended infants and ignored us. Sunburned, balding Americans with big grins went on talking across seat backs.

The man waiting just left of the boarding gate wore black trousers and a powder blue uniform shirt, open at the collar, with flap pockets, short sleeves, and shoulder boards. He had gold-rimmed spectacles, a soft, middle-aged face, a smile he could have been born wearing. "Do you have your passport?" he asked gently.

It was in a breast pocket, wrapped around the stubs of my El Al ticket. I handed over the whole thing. Large fingers held the pieces together as he looked at the photograph, read the name and description, never glancing at me to see if they fitted. He closed the passport, made no move to return it. "There is a matter we need to discuss with you," he said. "You have met Superintendent Alboker? Good. Would you come with us?"

He turned a little, nicely implying that I might want to heel.

"I've got a ticket for this flight," I said.

"Yes, we're sorry to inconvenience you. A matter has arisen." A mellow smile. I understood those things happened, didn't I?

"I'm also an American citizen," I said carefully, a syllable at a time. He could read what he wanted into that: If he messed with me, I would tell my congressman to cut off aid, or write a letter to the *Times* travel page, or take my next vacation in Egypt.

"We would not interfere with your plans," he said apologetically, "except that a matter has come up."

Alboker wanted to spar with me again. Or Warren Morgenstern had wired money to the PLO. Or they'd counted towels at the King David. I said, *"What's* come up?"

"A matter of someone's having been killed," he said.

I didn't react, except to shut up. So Esther had been right.

He said, "Inasmuch as you know this person, we hope you can help us."

We got into their car, which was parked outside the terminal door. By then I couldn't hold the question in any longer. I said, "Who was killed?"

They looked at me but didn't answer.

They hadn't hemmed me into the back seat. It would have been hard to fit a plainclothesman on either side and leave room for a broom. I opened the door and put a foot on the ground. "I said, 'Who got killed?' "

They didn't want a big fuss in public, not right there at the airport in the middle of other people's teary good-byes. There was no reason not to tell me. The uniformed man told me. His lips moved, making no sense.

I had an awful feeling I already knew. Not Harry. . . .

He was saying, ". . . a prominent businessman. Our information is you have met him. Mr. Levy?"

"Levy?"

"Yes, you've met. Mr. Dov Levy."

I nodded. "We've met."

One plainclothesman drove, while the uniformed man leaned over the seat back and asked questions. We left the brightly lighted terminal area. The road was busy but dark. "When did you meet?" he asked.

"Yesterday morning."

"Are you certain of that?"

Of course I was certain. I told him so and added, "I'd have seen him again this morning, but he wasn't at the office when I stopped by."

He didn't ask why I'd stopped by. He asked his next question in the same patient monotone as the others. "Do you know where we are going?"

"Jerusalem?" I guessed.

"No, Jerusalem is east of here." He waited for me to guess again, or to confess to having done in Dov Levy. He was so nice about it that if I'd killed anyone, I would certainly have told him.

"Do you recognize this road?"

If it had run past my apartment building in SoHo, I wouldn't have known so in this pitch. I was getting annoyed at his friendly invitations to incriminate myself. "You should ask your driver these questions," I said.

He turned me over to Alboker as soon as he could. The driver transferred my bags to the dry ground under fragrant trees where oranges hung fat and ripe. A few yards away, Dov Levy lay with his head caved in and several bullet wounds in the back for good measure. The police had set up powerful floodlights that left no shadow near the body, nowhere for the facts of death to hide. His skin had been swarthy, but the lights washed away all color except the garish ones. He lay mostly facedown, head angled slightly toward us. The visible eye was closed. Around him, the grass was stubby. A hand extended away from the body, knuckles against an orange.

Alboker stood within the perimeter of light, sharp face pinched. He gestured without looking at me. "You see, Mr. McCarry, this is not an act of terrorists."

I wondered how terrorists' victims looked different.

Alboker said, "Do you know a reason for this?"

"No." I didn't like looking at the body of the rumpled, disorganized man. But viewing the remains worked its intended effect on the suspect, loosening his tongue. "Do you know where his assistant is, Miss Sennesh?"

Not taking his eyes off the ground, Alboker said, "This is not a terrorist act. The man was killed for some prosaic, ugly, trivial reason. You were going to invest in his company, were you not?"

"No." I looked around. There were a dozen or so policemen and women on the scene, others walking among the trees in the distance. A half dozen vehicles hemmed the edge of the grove. Behind the black cover of trees, hills rose against the lighter black of the sky. We were high above the coastal plain. Despite the blazing floodlights, the air was cold. I wished myself back in Jerusalem; New York was too remote to wish for. Stuffing my hands into my blazer pockets, I stood looking at what the policeman wanted me to look at and shivered.

"I think you can help us," Alboker said. "You were not going to invest in his company, yet you told me yesterday that was why you had come to Israel. You were not going to invest, yet you visited with Levy on several occasions."

"One occasion. I considered investing in Agritech. Harry was a good salesman. One look at the operation cured me of the thought."

"You do not find Israeli companies attractive?" He turned his face on me for the first time.

"I don't know anything about most Israeli companies. And not much about Agritech. Just enough not to risk money in it."

"You are a shrewd man, I can see. Is it possible you had already made an investment in Agritech? Perhaps a small one? And you were angry with Mr. Brickman and Mr. Levy?"

"Why not a large one? And I wasn't just angry, I was furious." Whether it was the cold, or the sight of Dov Levy, my teeth had started rattling and the words came out broken.

"You did not see or visit with Mr. Levy today?"

"No."

He nodded. "It's unfortunate that someone saw you together this afternoon. It makes it very difficult for me to believe anything else you say."

"I didn't see Dov Levy this afternoon. Or this morning. Or this evening."

"You see him now, and I think you are denying the fact in front of you."

"You're entitled to your opinion."

"It is founded upon fact—and upon your lies. I must ask you to return to Jerusalem with us."

"Who says he saw me with Levy?"

He stared at me without answering, and I noticed that a uniformed officer had moved to either side of me. The van they put me in was no warmer than the outdoors, but at least I didn't have to look at Levy.

Alboker sat in front, next to his driver, just as his friendly colleague had done coming from the airport. There were differences during the forty-minute trip to police headquarters. Alboker never looked around, and he never spoke. The largish men on either side did their best to ignore me as well. The suspect had become baggage. You didn't interrogate baggage; you delivered it to its fate.

Alboker *disappeared at* the central police headquarters, and the two men put me in a room and left. The room was painted cinder block with a small square table, half a dozen chairs, a wall map showing police districts. It was a little upscale for an interrogation room, or they had nice ones. I sat and waited. They had let the suspect regret his crimes for only fifteen minutes, not enough to set a schoolboy babbling, when Alboker came in with another man.

"This is Inspector Shaltiel, of the Investigations Section," Alboker announced. "He is present because I believe we have a straightforward criminal matter, not a matter of state security."

Shaltiel, who was investigating my passport, ignored the introduction. He was gray-haired, with small hands, a military-style mustache, small blue eyes. "We shan't detain you needlessly, Mr. McCarry," he said. His inflections were a reminder that British public schools had once ruled the world. "About your meeting this afternoon with Mr. Levy, if there was a reason you felt it must remain confidential, surely you see now that our getting at the facts is more important."

He didn't quite hang a question on the end of that, so I didn't answer.

"And inasmuch as our information seems to conflict with yours, we want to resolve the differences so that we may get to the bottom of the matter. You *do* understand?" He asked it suddenly, as if it had just occurred to him that I might not.

"I did not see Dov Levy this afternoon."

"That is curious," he murmured. "But let's assume it's true. How did you spend the day?"

"I met an assistant of Mr. Levy's, a Miss Sennesh, and we had lunch."

"I see. What was the purpose of that meeting?"

"To see whether either of us had a brainstorm concerning Brickman, I suppose. He was the key investor in Agritech, bringing in his partners and clients. Without his support, the company's prospects are poor."

He hummed and clucked. "Where did you meet this assistant?"

"At Agritech's office."

"Was Mr. Levy present?"

"No."

"Where did you have lunch?"

"I don't know what the neighborhood's called. Over by the windmill."

"The neighborhood called Yemin Moshe?"

"It could be. I don't know."

"Did you return with her to Agritech's office?"

"No. We had hoped to see Harry's partner, who's in town, and do some more brainstorming." I was composing freestyle as I talked. "Warren, that's the partner, had other meetings and we never linked up. By the time we gave it up, it was time for me to head for the airport."

"And where did Miss Sennesh go then?"

"Probably home. Why don't you ask her?"

"We shall, of course."

There would be very little overlap in our stories, regardless of whether she improvised or told the truth. Any inconsistencies could be covered with apologies. Who could deny that the truth was indelicate? What bothered me wasn't the thought of Miss Sennesh contradicting me. I was worried because they didn't seem to have talked to her. If they had tried to find her and couldn't. . . .

"I'd have made that woman my first interview," I said.

Shaltiel looked unhappy.

"You haven't questioned her?"

"We shall," he said, "of course."

"I've nothing more to say. Please notify the embassy that you're detaining an American citizen."

They held a mumbled conference and left, letting a young officer keep me company.

I sat and stared at nothing as a knot grew in my chest. I hoped Esther hadn't gone back to the office.

113

* * *

The *door opened* again two hours later. I hadn't been sleeping, and for most of the time I hadn't been thinking about anything. The door opened, and I expected Shaltiel but it was Alboker. "Thank you for your cooperation, Mr. McCarry," he said. "You are free to leave."

I didn't move.

The baby-sitter, who had sprung to his feet, received a nod from Alboker and slipped out. The door swung wide. Behind Alboker, looking smaller in his shadow, stood Esther Sennesh. She wore a red-striped shirt and black denims, no trace of makeup, very little trace of an expression.

I got off the chair.

She gave me a businesslike nod. "We at Agritech regret your inconvenience, Mr. McCarry. I can drop you at your hotel."

Esther strode ahead of both Alboker and me, arms swinging with don't-mess-with-me authority. At the door, the baby-sitter was waiting with my bags. I collected them and headed outside. Alboker didn't bother to watch us leave. He disappeared past the reception desk. An urge to hurl something after him came and went.

The Agritech car sat in a bright sodium glare a few feet from the portico. Neither of us talked as Esther unlocked the car and I shoved my bags into the back. We got in, and she started the engine. "Tell me about Dov Levy," she ordered.

The street in front of the police building joined the Nablus Road, which took us into the center of the New City. As she drove, I gave her a sketchy account.

"How many times was he shot?"

"I don't know."

114

She didn't look away from the road. It was after midnight, but as we neared the hotel a few other cars appeared. She murmured, "More than once?"

"I don't know."

"Was he mutilated?"

"What?" The question left me at a loss. Mutilated? Bullets caused cosmetic damage, as well as ending a life. But it wasn't what she meant. She meant had they used knives on him after he was dead. I said, "No," and she drove on. She parked in the King David's lot and carried my shoulder bag. She hadn't asked me more questions. I had a few for her, but they could wait. The hotel had plenty of rooms even at one in the morning. We went up, dropped the luggage, and opened the windows. The room was at the back of the building, overlooking a garden. I phoned down and ordered a couple of tuna fish baguettes, a cheese platter, and four bottles of Gold Star.

Esther sat at the desk. The garden was empty, of course. So were the pool and the terrace. With the windows folded wide, a chill came in. She raised both hands and hid a yawn.

It wasn't the most sentimental reaction I could imagine for Dov Levy. Otherwise, I agreed. I threw my jacket onto a chair. I could feel the tension draining away. There hadn't been a day since my arrival when I hadn't dealt with soldiers, cops, or embassy lowlifes. There hadn't been more than half a day when someone or other hadn't tried pulling my leg.

"Esther," I said, "I'm sorry about your friend."

"Which one?"

"Let's say Dov at the moment. Why would somebody kill him?"

"Why would somebody kidnap Brickman?"

There was a knock at the door, and a waiter brought in a cart, set up the small table catercorner from the bed. I beck-

115

oned Esther over, poured a beer for her. Her emotional detachment wasn't a bad thing, but it made her useless in thinking about our problem. Raising my glass, I said, "We both need to sort this out."

She didn't respond.

"What are you going to tell the police when they ask about Agritech?" I said.

That got her attention, a little bit. "They asked tonight. I told them what we do—*did*, I guess would be closer. There does not seem to be a reason in that for Dov's murder."

"Your police are pretty gullible if they believe that."

"What do you mean?"

"Why do you think Levy was killed?"

"I am not sure. . . . I think they believe he may have been robbed. We have these crimes, too. The fact he was not mutilated. . . ."

"It's interesting," I said, "that Superintendent Alboker was about to step out of the picture. Without security implications, it wasn't his problem. But something got him interested again."

She shook her head.

Breaking off a piece of baguette, I said, "What did you tell them we did today?"

"I said I had shown you some archeological sites."

They might have decided I simply hadn't mentioned that part.

"What did we talk about?"

"Agritech finances. I said you were considering an investment."

They could have assigned that discrepancy to wishful thinking on her part.

"Why do you think they let me go?" I said.

"That is obvious. They accepted that I had been with you

all afternoon, and that you had no time to murder anyone." She cut a baguette in half, nibbled with no enthusiasm. "I do not know why they arrested you in the first place."

"They had a witness who saw me with Levy during the day. Or so they said."

"Nonsense. There cannot have been such a witness. Unless I can be mistaken for Dov. They were bluffing."

"Or the witness was anonymous, and they had to check it out. I don't know how the body was found. There was a guy from the embassy," I said, changing the subject, "who had a lot of questions about Agritech. Also questions about Harry."

"What do you expect? Brickman was missing. Wouldn't you ask what he had been doing?"

"Did the police give you any hint when Dov was killed?"

She looked at her plate, put the sandwich down, shook her head.

"What about when he was seen last?" I said.

She took a swallow of beer. "They did not tell me anything. They did not even mention that someone had implicated you."

They hadn't told her anything. They hadn't, it seemed, questioned her much. And when she gave an account of our day that didn't match my version, they nodded cheerfully and cut us both loose.

"Last night—the night before last, I mean—when you were at police headquarters with Morgenstern and Karen Brickman, I went for a walk. A white Mercedes hung around me. I think it was either the embassy or Superintendent Alboker keeping track. My bet is Alboker. If the watch was still on when I picked you up, Alboker knows we spent the day together and neither of us saw Dov." I paused. "You didn't see him earlier?"

She shook her head.

"If Alboker knows all that, why did he pull me in? And why hadn't they talked to you?"

"The last part I can answer. When we parted, I took a bus down to Tel Aviv. I have a friend who lives there. I arrived back at my parents' apartment only a few minutes before the police called. My mother was alarmed by then, because they had been calling every half hour."

"They told you Dov had been killed?"

"Not until I got to the headquarters. The other question you have—why they did not let you leave Israel—is not so mysterious, is it? The superintendent had a murder on top of a kidnapping, both at least possibly connected to terrorism. Even if his spies assured him you couldn't have killed Dov, you might have had information he could use."

"They could have come right out and asked, instead of pretending I was a suspect."

"Perhaps you are still a suspect, even though your hand did not fire the fatal shot. Or perhaps he hopes you have information but are reluctant to compromise a friend. There are many possibilities."

"Thinking a stockbroker wouldn't compromise a friend is a stretch."

"You should not make fun of yourself. It is unmasculine. Besides, I said there are many possibilities."

If I was right about Alboker's having assigned a watchdog, the white Mercedes would be on duty tonight. Mentioning that, I asked Esther if she wanted to confirm any suspicions they had by staying over.

"You make it so romantic," she said. "But we are not romantic, are we?" She had phoned her mother from the headquarters.

I rolled the dinner cart into the hall, hung out a DON'T DISTURB sign, and double-locked the door. Leaving the windows wide, I piled an extra blanket on the bed. On the verge of sleep, I realized I hadn't rescheduled with El Al, hadn't warned the office I'd been delayed, hadn't talked to my fiancée in three (or was it more?) days. The part of my mind that was still dealing with the outside world examined each of those derelictions and pronounced each in turn a matter of no consequence. Not even Esther's hip, tucked against my middle, held me back from the long silent stumble over the edge.

I *was asleep* less than ten minutes when the phone rang. I picked it up and knew, however fuzzy my brain felt, that I recognized the voice.

TEN

A *shock is* supposed to bring you awake suddenly and fully.
A half hour later, my mind was still drifting back toward
sleep. I was dressed, sitting in the passenger seat of
Agritech's Fiesta. Esther Sennesh was at the wheel. She was
alert, excited, eager to deal with the dark highway leading
through Arab towns. She had chattered away as we collected the car. It was a bad road that passed through Bethle-
hem and Hebron—except she called them Bet-Lehem and
Hevron, but then she called Jerusalem something like Yerushalayim. A rock or two might be thrown at us. The army
might very well stop us. But it would take at least an hour
more if we went west and picked up the highway that ran
through safe territory. Route 60 was the most direct way to
our destination, which was a place on the edge of the desert
called Beersheba.

Alboker's watchdogs had called it a night. We didn't spot
anyone waiting near the front door of the King David, and
we had the street to ourselves past the rail station and an

industrial area. The street became a highway, and the night closed in.

She drove with a heavy foot, slowing only as the road twisted through a small town, and then not slowing much. There wasn't much sign of life, an occasional light well back from the road. As the road straightened, she said, "That was Bet-Lehem. The rock throwers are sleeping with their donkeys."

"That's terrific," I said.

"You must be happy," she said, "even if you are not awake."

I rubbed my eyes, stared at the road, which had a habit of bending suddenly out of the reach of the headlights. It was warm in the car. I'd had the instinct, if not the presence of mind, to pull on a cotton sweater under my blazer. Even so our walk to the car park had frozen me. It couldn't have been more than thirty-five degrees in Jerusalem.

Esther was happy. Happy and agitated and eager.

Picking up the phone at that time in the morning had been a mistake. Calls after about one A.M. are never good news. At best you get wrong numbers dialed by combative drinkers. Otherwise . . . your brother's car went off the road, grandpa had a heart attack, mom's okay they think but you'd better catch a plane.

Or a voice from the dead.

I caught myself drifting off, sat up straighter, and gave the window crank a turn.

The voice on the phone didn't introduce itself. It just said, "I couldn't think of anyone else who could come and get me."

Even jerked from sleep, I recognized him. It was Harry Brickman.

Sitting up, I'd reached for the light, hadn't found it.

Harry Brickman's voice sounded very close. He could have been downstairs. The brashness I'd known was only a ghost. He said, "I've been through unbelievable shit. Can you come and get me?" When I didn't answer right away, he said, "I would go to the police, but I don't know who to trust right now."

"Where are you, and what happened?"

Esther had been stirring. Something in my tone brought her awake, and she found the light on her side and sat up. She mouthed, "Who are you talking to?"

Harry was going on at the other end. I covered the mouthpiece and told her, "You're not going to believe it. It's Harry—"

She threw herself at me, grabbing the receiver, and with her elbow on my chest and a breast jabbing at my eye, she assured herself that darling Brickman was indeed alive. After that it wasn't a question of whether she went and retrieved him but of whether I came along. She flung on her clothes, back turned, suddenly shy.

"He is in Beersheba, at a truckers' restaurant. I know the place; it's near the bus station. I did the last part of my national service near there."

"I'll wake Morgenstern and Mrs. Brickman," I said.

"No! If he'd wanted *them*, he'd have called *them*!"

"He doesn't know they're here."

"He called *us*," she said, and I didn't correct her.

He hadn't gotten around to telling her anything except where he was and, I gathered, a few feverish endearments. Esther hadn't mentioned that Karen was in town. I would enjoy giving him that news. Preferably when he'd just gotten comfortable with the thought of picking up where he'd left off with his Sabra.

There was nothing on the road. I'd started to yawn when Esther said, "If we have trouble, it will be just ahead."

"What's ahead?"

"Dahisha, a refugee camp," she said, putting the gutturals in with contempt so it came out D'hish'. "It's very dangerous if we are forced to stop."

"Is the camp right on the highway?"

"East of it, but there has been a lot of building outside the camp. And on the west side of the road, there is a stone quarry with millions of rocks."

We passed an army vehicle almost before I saw it, and she slowed. Two hundred yards farther, she stopped beside an armored vehicle, got out and said something to a soldier sitting on a fender. As they talked, another man in military gear appeared from across the highway. Esther gestured vaguely south.

When she got back in the car, Esther said, "At least we won't have trouble with the army farther down the road."

"Why would we?"

"It is not wise to drive fast through here. They are suspicious of speeding cars and do not always ask permission before shooting. The other posts will be expecting us."

"So they won't shoot?" I said, just to hear myself. Off the road, lights came on and another armored vehicle I hadn't seen moved onto the highway ahead of us. Esther put the car into gear and followed.

"We have an escort past Dahisha," she said.

"How did you manage that?"

"My uncle was in a unit that administered this area. They remember him."

The army vehicle led the way for what couldn't have been more than a few miles before easing onto the shoulder. Esther flashed the lights and swung past. "We really should not have come on this road, but that was the worst. It should be okay until Yatir, and then we will have another escort. Up ahead on the right, the lights are Gush Etzion."

"Another Arab camp?"

"No, it was a Jewish settlement for many years. During the War of Independence, the Arabs took it." Her voice dropped away. "Some of the children of the settlers came back after the Six Days War. My uncle was among them. Now there are farms again, and a yeshiva, and the settlers run this road in convoys like the old days."

I tried a little math. The War of Independence as she called it had been fought in 1948. I said, "Some of the first settlers must be a little old for rough stuff."

"None of the earlier settlers are here."

"They didn't come back?"

"They didn't leave. Some were killed. The others surrendered, and they were killed. That is why one does not surrender."

A bit later she met another armored escort and we blew through Hebron like a summer storm. Forty minutes after that, Esther announced we were in the outskirts of Beersheba. She hadn't said much after passing the last armored car. Hebron was an Arab city but had been a center of Jewish scholarship until a massacre in 1929. She told me that and fell silent. The light above the land told me something was ahead before Esther said it was Beersheba. We passed from barren hills into cultivated fields, then scattered industrial buildings, then apartment buildings. We passed the bus station, and the truckers' stop was a block further, across the street from a single-storey strip of shops.

Harry looked worse for three days' absence. His right cheek was a swollen fruit of yellow and black that left only a slit for the eye. A scabbing-over patch of raw skin reached most of the way across his forehead. His lower lip was split just left of center. His face and arms were sunburned an angry red that looked bronze in the diner's yellow light. His tightly curled blond hair might have been bleached a few shades lighter, but it was so dirty I couldn't tell. He was still wearing the pink plaid shirt and khakis he'd worn three mornings ago, both now spattered brown with blood. His knuckles were skinned, one finger blackened from congested blood. He didn't smile when he saw us. He barely lifted his head. He was sitting at a table under a blue and yellow cardboard sign with large Hebrew letters on top and the word *Hashomron* below and the price 9.70 on the side. He looked like he was having trouble staying awake.

Esther cried out something unintelligible and ran to him. He held her at bay with an elbow. She petted his neck, looked down to the parts he was protecting.

"I think a couple of ribs are cracked," he said. "Uh, listen, can one of you give the counterman twenty shekels for the phone call?"

I paid the counterman and came back. "What happened?" I said.

"That's a dreary story I'm too pooped to tell."

"When did they let you go?"

He gave his head half a shake, which may have been all he could manage. "Let's get the hell out of here," he wheezed.

Instead of arguing about his condition, Esther helped him to his feet. He walked pretty well. His left knee, where the slacks were ripped, was stiff. He let his arm rest on Esther's shoulder as if it felt pretty good there. We eased him into the front seat, and I climbed into the back from the driver's side.

"We will be in Yerushalayim in ninety minutes," she said.

"Not yet," Harry said. "Let's find a hotel."

"But you need a hospital, *hamoudi*."

"I've had cracked ribs before. A hotel, that's what I need."

125

She got us checked into a motor court near the university, explaining Harry as an American rock hound who had taken a spill in the desert. Harry grinned, convincingly prone to stupidities like that. He'd also left his identification at his hotel in Eilat. His name was Gunderson. We got a single large room with four beds. Harry sat on the corner of one. I watched him. His pudgy face had shrunk in the last few days, except for the bruised parts. Between his knees, his hands trembled.

Esther knelt beside him, with a glass of water. "If you have been exposed, you need this."

He drank slowly. The truck drivers who had finally picked him up had let him empty two Thermoses of lemonade. The counterman had let him drink his fill of water.

"So they let you go," Esther coaxed.

"Not exactly." Harry let her take the glass before lying back. He winced as the ribs grated.

"What happened, *hamoudi?*"

"I think I killed one of them." His voice slurred. He began snoring.

He *slept until* almost noon. Esther and I argued over calling Morgenstern and Karen Brickman, the police, and the embassy. "What will a few more hours matter?" she said. "Brickman told you he didn't know who to trust."

"He was out of it when he said that. And since when don't you trust your own police?"

"I do trust them. So will Brickman when he recovers."

She went out an hour and a half later, when it was getting light, for groceries. Most of the time she sat near Harry, refusing to look at me. Her memory had become an embarrassment. The situation wasn't as awkward or as complicated as she thought, but I didn't want to hurt her feelings by saying so.

I dumped my jacket on the farthest bed, took my shoes off, and stretched out. Only a floor lamp near the door was switched on. I closed my eyes but had too many questions breezing around in my head to sleep. If Harry and I had been alone, he wouldn't have slept until I had answers.

When Esther went out, the room was getting bright through gaps in the draperies. As soon as the door closed, I surprised myself by dropping off. She must have been back some time when I awoke. There were cups and butcher's paper on the bed nearest me. On the bed next to Harry, Esther was curled up, an arm across her eyes, rope of hair across a shoulder. Harry Brickman was sitting up, bare feet crossed, with a baguette of some kind on his lap. He said softly, "There's hummus, if you want it, chum. Don't wake her. She's exhausted."

I wondered if bouncing his head off a door a few times would wake her. If it did, she would find some fault about my treatment of *Hamoudi* the Invalid. I used the toilet, washed my face, came out, and put my shoes on. It occurred to me that nothing was stopping me from calling the police, except the McCarry family's inbred disposition against doing things like that.

I sat at the room's single table, which was small and round and chipped, and looked into a container of pale, grainy hummus. Wondering which end of a camel it had come out of, I pushed the container away, opened a bottle of Orangina. Without looking at him, I said, "What happened to you, Harry?"

"Somebody's mighty pissed off at Agritech."

I thought of a couple of things to say. *Your investors should be.* Or: *Have you run that idea past Dov Levy?* We hadn't told

127

him about Levy. What I actually said was milder. "Can you think why anyone should be?"

"No . . . except the Arabs hate anything that would make Israel more prosperous."

From what I'd seen of Dov Levy's business plan, the Arabs should have been cheering on Agritech. It didn't look like a money-maker in my lifetime. "There are some things you should know," I said, "and quite a few I want to know. You can go first. What happened after they ambushed us?"

"They gagged and blindfolded me pretty fast. We drove west, I think it was west, for quite a while. Somewhere we changed to an open-back truck. I was in the back with a couple of them, with crates of oranges stacked on all sides. I think we came south through Israel; the roads were busy." They had settled in at a place somewhere in the Negev, a place that felt and sounded remote. They kept him hooded and tied. He never glimpsed their faces, never heard them utter a word. They didn't abuse him, but they fed him and gave him water only once in the space of two days. Most of the time he thought he was alone, or with one guard. They had him lie on an army-style cot, canvas on a wooden frame. Yesterday morning, using his own blood for lubrication, he had slipped one wrist free of his bonds. He was too weak and unsteady to do more than hobble. He hobbled behind a door—he was in a windowless, linoleum-floored room—and when a guard came to check on him he used a section of camp cot on the man's neck. His swings felt ineffectual, so long after the man was down he kept hammering his neck and head, constantly afraid the heavily built man would shake off the blows and get back to his feet.

When a stream of blood poured out of the man's ear, Harry decided he could stop the beating. He was half-crazed with thirst. The house was empty except for Harry and the guard. It had two bedrooms, a living room, and eating corner that shared space with a kitchen. The windows were curtained with torn pieces of bed sheets. He hesitated a long time before picking a window at the back of the larger bedroom, where he pulled a corner of the curtain aside. He saw a bare yard with a small dead tree, scraps of metal, and hard-packed earth. It was a frustrating view, because a concrete block wall enclosed the living room entrance and limited his range of sight to about thirty degrees. He went to a window in the living area that faced the opposite direction and moved the bed sheet only enough to see past the window frame. Here he could see a small concrete patio, an untrimmed brown bush of some sort, and as he enlarged his field of vision, junk scattered across a sandy yard: a wheel housing; a white metal cabinet; large food cans; other things that didn't register.

What he saw beyond filled him with hope at first, then despair. Widely spaced and set at odd angles, so that none directly faced another, were several more houses that looked much like this one would from the outside. He had thought immediately of the houses as a source of help, then recognized that the inhabitants were more likely to be enemies than friends. Nobody was visible, either close by or in the distance. For a few minutes, neither fact mattered to him. His chances of escape had shrunk to invisibility.

Wrapped in depression, he went back to the doorway of the smaller bedroom. He had thought of his captors as Arabs. He looked at the man on the floor, who wasn't moving. Despite his fear, he stepped closer. The man was a few inches over six feet, Harry guessed, and thickly muscled. He had a dense black beard but light, European features. He didn't look to Harry like an Arab.

He had a horrible thought then. The man *wasn't* an Arab, he was an Israeli come to Harry's rescue.

But if that was so, where were the other rescuers?

He had to acknowledge the possibility that he had made a mistake, but he thought it more likely that Arab or not, the man had been one of his captors. If he had searched the bedroom, he might have found evidence—a ski mask, a gun, even his own passport and wallet. But when he looked from the living room window again, it struck him odd that nobody at all was in sight. He watched for five minutes, moving from window to window. In between, he checked the man in the bedroom, got close this time, and concluded there probably wasn't any reason to investigate a third time. He wasn't a doctor, but he was pretty certain the man had stopped breathing.

He went out the door that offered the sheltering wall. It turned out there were houses on this side of the building that had been hidden from his line of sight at the window. He crouched in the shade and watched the houses. He had trouble concentrating. It had been hot in the house, but it was worse outside. The air was a dry, searing, motionless weight. He hadn't had anything to drink in at least twelve hours, nothing to eat in a day and a half. He knew that his thinking wasn't top-notch. He knew that if he made a mistake, he would be just as dead as if his abductors had used their guns. He had to control his desperate urge to run, his dread of the other captors' return. Deciding what to do, and in what sequence, took all his concentration. When he finally had it sorted out, his first objective was reconnaissance. His opportunities were limited by the fear there might be someone camped in one of the houses, although he was pretty certain the settlement was abandoned. *Supposed* to be abandoned, he corrected, although it also felt abandoned. His instincts on those matters were probably worth little, he knew. So his scouting consisted of looking everywhere he could from the small court, both on hands and knees as he peered around corners, and standing on a produce crate he dragged from inside as he looked over the top of the wall. When he was done he was fairly heartened on one count and disappointed on another. There was no sign that he could identify, absolutely none, of recent inhabitation. Nor was there a car or truck in sight, which meant he would have to walk. They had left him with his guard, and the two of them were meant to stay until the people with the truck returned. That could be very soon, but his concern was fading, a fact he attributed partly to physical lethargy. Reconnoitering done, he took his time putting together food and water. The house had no electrical service and no running water. His abductors, apparently laying in for a long siege, had wisely decided not to use the toilet. Harry observed no such constraint. There was no fresh food in the place except sticks of bread that ants had found. A countertop held bottles of Vichy water and soft drinks, canned fruit and vacuum-wrapped meat. He drank a bottle of water while looking for something to serve as a rucksack. He finally risked removing the section of bed sheet from the sheltered door's window, put together two bottles of water and the meat, and tied the sheet's ends together. Hooked on two fingers, the bundle sat just over his shoulder, not too comfortably. A third bottle he carried in his other hand.

In all likelihood, he could have walked boldly out the front door, followed the worn blacktop street in its broad loop to where it became a once-graveled but now-bare dirt track that promised, somewhere across the desert, to meet a highway. Instead, he crept out the sheltered door, inched around the house on hands and knees, and crossed the yard in a hunched dash that left him breathless in seconds. By the time he cleared the settlement, he was trudging upright, indifferent in his exhaustion to whether he was seen or not. He was happy nonetheless. No one had cried out, no one had given chase, and no one had shot him.

"I'd had worse mornings on Wall Street," Harry said. "Thing is, it was just so fucking hot I knew I wasn't going to make it."

From the sun's position, he knew it was relatively early in the day. But the air was over one hundred degrees and so dry that even as he had run from the house he hadn't felt any sweat. He'd never been in a desert before, but he knew that if he remained exposed, his body would give up its moisture at an alarming rate. He couldn't see that he had much choice. He followed the dirt road. He tried to stay alert, knowing he might have a few seconds' warning if anyone drove onto the road. But he had trouble keeping his mind on that thought. Mainly he focused on how much the heat hurt his head.

When he was about a quarter mile from the highway, he caught a flash ahead like an explosion. It was sunlight hitting the windshield of a vehicle turning off the main road. He overreacted and threw himself down a four-foot embankment into a dry wadi. He collected a few scrapes and lay on his hands with a broken lip dripping blood onto the ground. He had fallen in the right spot. An outcrop of rock hid him from view as they approached, and the wall of the embankment was so steep that a passenger in the vehicle would have had to look straight down at exactly the right moment to see him. He watched from his peripheral vision, afraid to allow even his eyes to move. The vehicle that rumbled past, with three men sitting tall in the seats, was an open jeep indistinguishable from the one we'd encountered on the road to Shomrim Tsion. He could see little of the men's faces. One could have been an Arab. He didn't think the others were.

The worst part of their return was that he couldn't move openly on the highway hoping for rescue. At least not until he had put some distance between himself and this place. They would come looking for him.

When he reached the highway, it was empty. By then he thought he knew where he was, more or less. Behind the abandoned settlement, ragged hills led up to broken walls of mountain. The first hills were probably miles away, but the effect was one of being at their feet. In the evening, if he was right about directions, shadows would flow down from the mountains across this barren valley.

Ahead, perhaps a mile past the highway and running parallel to it, was a blazing white flatland where water glinted, and on the far side were red mountains. He had never been here before, but he had mentioned this direction to me as we headed for Shomrim Tsion. The highway was the north-south Number 90 that ran along the Dead Sea on the border with Jordan and then continued all the way south to Eilat. Harry thought he was close to the bottom of the Dead Sea—there was less water ahead than salt flat— and that told him that somewhere, not too many miles from where he stood, there were roads climbing out of this deep valley (the lowest point of land on earth was the Dead Sea, he remembered). The lowest and the hottest, he thought. If he guessed right about the location of those roads, he would have high ground from which to size up approaching traffic and select rescuers. He guessed that at least one road lay north of him. He wished he had read the maps of the area more carefully.

His most serious injury, the cracked ribs, came two hours later for no reason except that the ground slid away under his foot and he fell on the bundle. It took him an hour to get back onto his feet. For part of that time, he thought he wouldn't. The sun had drained his energy. Breathing was difficult. There was no shade. He became certain that he would lie there, even after the agony in his side had ebbed, even after the sun had passed its zenith, and he knew he would be dead long before nightfall. He tried to fasten on something to get him moving. He tried to picture Esther's face and couldn't. He tried to remember her breasts and couldn't. But he decided to get up anyway, and to stay far enough off the highway that his abductors wouldn't see him.

He found shade under a rock shelf a half mile back from the road. He ate packaged sausage and drank the last of his water. The highway had few travelers. Occasionally, a small truck would appear to the north, coming out of a corkscrew descent, or a compact car, most often white. Once a military truck rolled north, followed by a jeep. Harry stayed under his rock.

To the north lay a deep gorge, or *makhtesh*, cut through the chalky earth. Whatever happened, he couldn't go very far in that direction. To the south, he could just see the bare road to the settlement. He had lifted his head from between his knees when the plume of rising dust caught his eye. The jeep already had reached the highway. It was sitting there, like a dog at the edge of a sidewalk, arguing with itself about which way smelled more promising.

For a minute, Harry entertained a hope. The men in the jeep wouldn't know that he hadn't been rescued. They wouldn't know how long they had before the army or the police began searching these roads. The men in the jeep might be looking for a way of escape rather than for a lost prisoner.

When they turned onto the highway and headed north, the hope evaporated. The jeep moved very slowly. Without being able to see well, he knew that at least one of the men was scanning the desert, perhaps with binoculars, looking for him.

He was safe under his rock shelf.

The jeep passed, and he waited in the withering heat. He happened to look out, not certain whether he had been asleep or not, sometime later as the vehicle passed his shelter again, heading south. He didn't move. Sometime in the afternoon, a truck joined the search. Harry was too sick to care. He almost hoped they would find him.

They gave up in the late afternoon. An hour passed without his seeing the patient hunt, and he suspected they'd abandoned it. Another hour or so later, he felt confident that was the case. It took him ninety minutes to totter across the thousand yards separating him from the highway. He fell three times. The worst of the sun's heat had passed, but he was exhausted, dehydrated, and close to heatstroke. From the roadside, he tried flagging down a speeding Audi, but the filthy, bloody-faced apparition sent the driver swerving to the center of the road where he accelerated. It was a small delivery truck, following behind, that stopped after he collapsed halfway onto the pavement.

"Two Arab guys," Harry said. "They gave me lemonade and took me to Beersheba. They didn't speak English, and my Hebrew isn't very good. But they knew the word 'hospital.' That's where they wanted to take me. I got the idea across I'd had a hiking accident and would be fine if they let me off anywhere in Beersheba. It was almost dark by then. There's a park over by the university. I crashed there, figuring I'd sleep an hour. I woke up after midnight and found the dump I called you from."

Esther had woken at some point during his account. She lay on the bed, arms under the pillow, eyes glittering with tears.

"Why didn't you call the police as soon as you were safe?" I said.

"My thinking wasn't great. I couldn't get it straight with myself: What would happen if I went to the police?"

"You're usually not muddleheaded," I said.

"I don't usually get my brains baked," he said. "It wasn't just that. The guy I hit . . . I don't know what it means. He was wearing an army uniform."

ELEVEN

"They sell those in hundreds of surplus stores," Esther objected. "Everybody in Israel owns old army uniforms. I have mine. What does it prove?"

"It doesn't prove anything," Harry conceded. "But it makes me wonder."

"About what?" I said.

"What if they were army. Maybe not even acting officially. Just a few assholes working on their own, trying to create an incident. Something that would get blamed on the Arabs."

"Motek, you were out in the sun too long." Esther slid from one bed to the other, touched his head gently while inspecting it for knotholes. "The army has no need to create incidents that will be blamed on Arabs. The Arabs create them every day."

"Apart from the uniform, Harry, is there some reason you think it was the army?" I watched both of them, as much curious about Esther's reaction as his.

She kept petting his head. He gave a drawn-out "No-o-o . . ."

"Did they say anything to you?"

"Not a fucking word the whole time. They didn't speak among themselves where I could hear. You see? I was supposed to look at those masks and T-shirts and think 'Palestinians' or 'terrorists.' "

"It is still the most likely answer," Esther said.

Remembering the skepticism of both the army and the police, I said, "Could they have been Israelis?"

"What have I been telling you?"

"I mean, Israeli civilians?"

"Same old question—'Why?' I haven't done anyone here any dirt, haven't screwed around with anybody's wife." He removed Esther's hand, shrugged.

She said, "Something terrible happened in Jerusalem. I do not want to tell you, but . . ."

"Just a minute," I said. "Harry, what do you think they planned to do with you?"

"How would he know if they said nothing?" Esther said.

"I just want his impression."

"Well . . . they kept me blindfolded. . . ." His battered round face turned hopeful. "That's supposed to be a good sign, isn't it? I couldn't identify them."

I wasn't sure it mattered.

His tentative smile had already vanished. "Fuck it. They were going to kill me. That's what I think. I was a parcel, and sooner or later it's easier to bury the parcel."

"You can't know that," Esther said.

"I don't know it, sweetheart. The question was my impression, and that's my impression. Now, what happened in Jerusalem?"

He looked from one of us to the other. Esther finally said, "Dov Levy was murdered yesterday. It's horrible. He was my father's friend. The police questioned Donald, because someone said they saw them together. It was a lie, and I told them. We were together."

"Trying to figure why you'd been snatched," I said, but he showed no sign of wondering. If his brain had gotten a good cooking in the desert, he might never ask why Esther had been in my room at one o'clock in the morning.

"Levy—why would anyone kill Levy?" Harry said.

"The police think a mundane reason, conventional crime or passion," I said. "It's quite a coincidence, though. You're kidnapped, Levy is murdered. You're both involved with Agritech Consultants."

He scratched his chin, which wore three days of yellow bristle. He glanced at Esther, who was sitting on the edge of the bed. "There must be other things we have in common. We're both Jewish. Hell, we both know Esther!"

"So do I, and so do her family and friends." I couldn't read the look that passed between them. I was getting suspicious of Harry. He didn't know why he'd been nabbed. Couldn't imagine why Dov Levy had been murdered. Dismissed the most visible connection between events, Agritech Consultants. I said, "Levy gave you a business plan for Agritech, didn't he?"

"A business plan?"

"You don't remember?"

"Well . . ."

"He said it was in a blue-bound book. He wanted it back. Esther and I looked through your place and couldn't find it. Do you know what I'm talking about?"

He felt his scraped forehead. The sun had gotten to him something just awful, left him confused about what he'd seen and what he hadn't, muddleheaded about everything—but still able to outsmart his friend McCarry. He sighed. "It doesn't ring a bell."

139

"Esther thought you had it," I said. She couldn't jump to his rescue without spoiling their game. "We searched your house and couldn't find it. Then Avis found it in their car. You'd been carrying it that morning. They sent it over to me at the hotel. I couldn't make head or tail of it as a business plan."

He didn't give a big giggle and say, *"Oh, that business plan!"* He cleared his throat and said, "Actually, that document is supposed to be confidential. What did you do with it?"

I ignored the question. "I read your private placement memo in New York. This version sounds like a different company. You had projections of doubling and redoubling in revenue, high profit margins, and returns to your investor group of forty percent annually. That's what I remember, anyway. You can contradict me if you want to. No? Then I pore over Dov Levy's blue notebook and see references to a guaranteed return of nine percent. So I wonder: Is it the same Agritech?"

They looked at me, both of them, like the Ma and Pa of the carnival midway when the mark's beefing about the two-headed mule. *Sure it's stuffed, but honest to hell that second head wasn't sewn on.*

"It's complicated," Harry said, "a little bit."

"Most good scams are."

He looked pained. Not innocent, though. "I wouldn't invite you in on a scam, chum. Who knows, Agritech might return forty percent. And if it doesn't, nobody gets hurt. The main thing is, that blue book is real sensitive. If you didn't return it to Levy—"

"Warren Morgenstern has it," I said. "Or maybe he's done reading it and turned it over to your wife. That's your wife, Karen, mother of Little Aaron." I didn't give a hoot about his family life, his faithfulness, or Little Aaron, upon whom I'd never laid eyes. But a cheap shot was better than no shot at all.

"Oh, shit," he muttered. Rather than thrash around for a strategy, he decided right off how to deal with the situation. "Esther, sweet, you tell Don all he wants to know about Agritech. I'm going to take a shower."

He headed into the bathroom. Water roared.

The afternoon must have been heating up, because the room's air conditioner seemed to be falling behind. I got up and jiggled the setting until a slightly cooler breeze accompanied louder hammering. After that I went around the room screwing up food wrappers and dropping them in the waste can.

"He will need new clothes," Esther said. "I will go out and get something."

"You've been told to fill me in on Agritech."

"He does not tell me what to do," she said. "I will tell you as we shop. It is not complicated."

I banged on the door and asked Harry his pant and shirt sizes. He shouted back, "Thirty-eight, twenty-eight, no cuffs; seventeen and a half, thirty-two."

I muttered "Jesus Christ" with enough feeling that Esther looked alarmed. "I was worried he would want cuffs," I explained.

Even high on a plateau, Beersheba was hot. Nothing like the desert poor Brickman had suffered in, Esther assured me—nothing like Yam Ha-Melah, the Dead Sea, she corrected herself, because technically the Negev Desert extended all the way to Beersheba even though it was under successful cultivation. "The Arid Zone Research Institute is at Beersheba; that's where Agritech has obtained some of its technology," she said. We found a low-ceilinged shop where Esther, translating Harry's measurements into metric, selected a pair of gray slacks, a cotton shirt, and underwear. She stopped at a pharmacy and bought a roll of surgical tape for his ribs. At the corner, I got a *schwarma*, a sandwich of lamb on a pita, to make up for the hummus. On a bright weekday afternoon, the town looked busy and prosperous. I didn't trust my eye on such things, but it looked like a large part of the population was Arab, perhaps Bedouin; the faces were long and bronzed. Esther walked with the purchases under her arm. "The technology we have is good, Mr. McCarry, because we have been at it a long time. Israelites were attempting to develop the Negev under King Uzziah seven hundred years before Christianity rose."

"Are you sure?" I said.

"Of course I am sure."

"We don't know what happened to your friend Dov twenty-four hours ago, or who kidnapped Harry three days ago, and we may never get the answers. But you say you know what King Uzziah's minions were doing twenty-seven hundred years ago."

"There are records."

"Inscribed, perhaps, by someone pushing for a federal grant. You can believe every word."

"There are also relics, *yadidi*," she said. I wondered where *yadidi* ranked among terms of affection. "Not all of history is a lie."

I couldn't argue archeology with her. Besides, maybe the relics *had* been used in an ancient effort to transform the desert. I couldn't prove they hadn't.

We had walked several blocks. Traffic at the next intersection was waiting for the passage of a small train of camels, which seemed to be having second thoughts as two Bedouin women struggled with their leads. A policeman was trying to help. Esther watched without interest until she saw me grinning. If she'd visited New York, the sight of a midtown cross street at high noon, with trucks and taxi cabs snarled three blocks deep, might have struck her as funny. She took my hand. "There is a camel market on Thursday mornings," she explained.

A block farther, a park with wilted palms took up about forty square feet. There was just enough room for us and a few birds. We sat on the only bench.

"I will tell you about Agritech Consultants," she said, "but you must agree not to tell Brickman's partners or his wife."

"Warren Morgenstern has the business plan. He may already have figured it out."

"You saw the plan and you haven't."

"Don't be too sure. In any case, Morgenstern's had longer to read it. He's also been hearing Harry's song on Agritech longer. Something that wouldn't mean much for me might click with him."

"You argue everything, like a lawyer!"

"Let's leave it at this. I won't tell them unless I have to. I won't tell them just to tell them."

"That is not good enough."

"It's better than my having a long talk with the cops."

She considered. "I will trust you."

"Start with the nine percent guaranteed return. Agritech's promise by itself wouldn't be worth anything. If the company flops, the guarantee is worthless. So who is backing up the deal?"

"Let me tell you how it came about. Dov Levy had the idea for the company. Producing food in harsh climates was a subject dear to him. He had contacts at the institute here and at the universities. To Dov, Agritech was a very practical project. He was not the kind of man you are, concerned only with the financial questions of business."

"Was he concerned about the financial questions at all?"

"Yes, of course. He knew the company would be successful but it would take several years to begin earning money. In the meantime, money would be flowing out and there would be no profit for the investors. That was a problem for Brickman, too, you see. He believes in Israel, but he has obligations to his investors."

"Harry was involved early?"

"Yes. The idea of the company was Dov's, but knowing his financial limitations he turned to Brickman for help. That was much more than a year ago."

"How did they meet?"

"Brickman was studying history on his visits to Israel. A professor at Hebrew University brought them together. Brickman told Dov what he would need to bring in American investors. Dov went to various ministries until he found one that was willing to help."

"What kind of help?"

"Brickman said he could bring in American money for Agritech if there was a—a—he called it a 'safety net.' He wouldn't ask anyone to guarantee his investors forty percent a year, but he said a new business like Agritech takes years to develop, is terribly risky, and he needed an assurance that his investors wouldn't get hurt."

"So a government ministry promised to provide the safety net?" I said.

"A guarantee of nine percent a year to American investors."

"Which ministry?"

"Economic Development. They have responsibility for attracting investment to Israel."

"Do they usually guarantee investors a nine percent profit?"

"I don't know."

"Did Harry say why he wasn't mentioning the guarantee to his investors?"

"He may have. He said they weren't the kind of people who buy Israel bonds."

I couldn't suppress a smile. I knew, and he'd known, that was exactly what they were getting.

He *was sitting* at the room's table, wearing towels around his waist and over his shoulders and eating the last of the hummus. There was a deep yellow and black bruise across his lower right rib. He looked less like he'd just been rolled under a truck, but the scrapes and bruises were more garish without the covering of grime. He gave me a round, tentative smile.

I said, "Did it ever occur to you that what you were doing is illegal?"

His shoulders rose a little, somewhere between acknowledgment and a shrug. "A few minor omissions in the offering circular . . ."

"A few key facts left out. Your clients could sue you for fraud. They could get a U.S. Attorney to have you indicted."

"C'mon, Donald. I was looking out for my people. I just didn't tell them how."

"You were dangling forty percent a year under their greedy noses when the thing's so rickety it may not be around next year. It's fraud, Harry. You got people to invest under false pretenses." When he let that go by, I said, "Why did the Ministry of Economic Development guarantee the deal? Agritech looks like a loser. Not even Israel thinks you make money backing belly flops."

"We have the technology," Esther protested.

"And you're selling it to deadbeats with unstable governments. Good luck."

"There's a chance the company will turn profitable,"

—

Harry said, "if the first projects work and other countries see what a difference Agritech can make in feeding their populations."

I stared at him. Selling stocks for a living, I associate with a lot of habitual liars. The best ones don't get tangled up in their own sales pitch. My colleague Timmy Upham says a dog turd with a big story still stinks, but he can sell a lot more of it. Harry talked as if he half-believed the story he'd been selling.

"There's no chance it'll earn you forty percent a year," I said. Noticing they'd distracted me from my question, I said, "Why *did* the Ministry of Economic Development back your scheme?"

"That's um . . . classified," he said, wearing his uneven smile.

"Classified by whom?"

"The government of Israel."

"You asshole," I said.

Esther handed him her purchases and sagged onto the other chair. "He'll figure it out," she said, "if he hasn't already. You might as well tell him."

"Agritech can earn this country standing in the Third World," Harry said. "That is worth something to the government."

"Sure. Standing in Ethiopia must be worth a bundle."

"If the technology works there, it could be a model for *dozens* of other countries."

"When you are under siege like Israel, you need friends," Esther added.

I wondered if I was getting sixty percent of the truth even then. If the government had one finger in Dov Levy's company, why not two or three? With people on the ground in enough Third World countries, all of them tied by satellite and computer to Jerusalem, Agritech and its friends in the government could pick up a lot of information about any trouble that might be brewing. What they might do with the information was another question. It could be a tradable commodity to someone—either a local party in interest who abhorred disorder, or a sidelined player who recognized disorder's opportunities. It would also be a good way to keep track of mischief against the home front. If I remembered news stories correctly, anti-Israel terrorists passed through obscure addresses on their way to work. If the Israeli intelligence service owned a point or two of Agritech's guarantee, would either Esther or Harry know it?

"I suppose there are other benefits," I said.

Neither of them jumped on the topic.

Harry disappeared into the bathroom with his new clothes. Besides being grateful that he was shy, I wanted to hear what Esther would say. She just sat, looking unhappy. I tried to sympathize. A friend of hers was dead. A project that had fanned her patriotic fires was doomed. A lover's wife was just up the highway. I said, "None of that tells us why Harry was kidnapped, or why Dov was killed."

She shook her head.

Sitting next to her, I said, "Unless the Finance Ministry or the Central Bank or some agency like that got wind of the deal . . . and decided having you all killed would save the country's economy."

"That is meant to be funny?"

"We'd better talk to the police, Esther. They'll be wondering where we are."

She nodded. "And Yigal Martin."

"Who?"

"The deputy minister of Economic Development. He approved the arrangement with Dov. He will have to make good on the guarantee for Brickman's early investors." She saw I wasn't following and said: "We have spent most of the money, and it will be years before anything comes to fruition. So that money is gone, and when Agritech closes, Yigal Martin will have to make it up, plus the nine percent."

"How much?"

"Several million dollars."

My mind wasn't exactly boggled, but I was glad I wasn't the deputy minister for Economic Development.

While Harry paced glumly, objections ignored, Esther called Superintendent Alboker in Jerusalem. From the snatches I heard, the voice on the other end was calm, courteous, surprised but not disbelieving. Or maybe he just sounded that way in Hebrew. Esther put down the phone. "He says that I am a moron—a water buffalo, to be exact—but he will not have me arrested. We are to return to Jerusalem and he will speak to Brickman. Take off your shirt. I will tape your ribs."

Harry muttered. If he was thinking cop thoughts, he was wondering if Alboker found it too convenient that the abductee had freed himself the day Dov Levy was murdered. Esther and I took our turns in the bathroom. I wasn't sure how much sleep I'd had in the last forty-eight hours. Not enough. My eyes felt gritty. My face was whiskery and disreputable looking: more shifty than usual. A shower helped. A razor would have taken care of everything but the shifty look. As Esther closed the door and the shower ran, Harry leaned across the table and said, "What did she tell you about Agritech?"

"You know what she told me. That Levy set it up to—"

"No, about *how* it was being run. Did she say anything about the money?"

"The Ministry of Economic Development is on the hook for a few million."

148

"No! About where the money *went!*" He was talking softly, glancing at the bathroom door. "That company can't have spent three-point-four million, which is the number, in twelve months. It just can't have. But that's what the bank accounts say. I'd asked Dov for the books, and all he'd coughed up was this so-called business plan."

"Wait a minute. You were still touting Agritech to me three days ago. You were trying to suck me into a company where you didn't trust the books?"

"Take it easy. I didn't know we had a problem till the evening before you arrived. After that, having you here was handy window dressing. I wouldn't have let you put the money in. But while we were flashing it around, I thought I could figure out what had happened to our cash."

His blue eyes and round face were sincere, almost enough to make me believe him.

"Once I wised up that those assholes holding me weren't Arabs, I figured they were working for Dov. I thought so right up until I coldcocked that jerk and saw the army clothes. Then I didn't know what to think."

"But until then?"

"Somebody had run through a load of cash, and I assumed they didn't want me talking."

"What does Esther say?"

"I didn't tell her. She handles Agritech's administration. I wasn't sure about her."

"And now?"

He gave me a pinched, uncomfortable look. "I don't know."

"Before we just turn up in Jerusalem, do you want to call your wife?"

"Sure, sure. Just call like that? It'd be less of a shock if you called. You know, worked her up to it. 'Grandma fell off the roof but guess what?' "

I tried the King David. Neither Mrs. Brickman's room nor Warren Morgenstern's answered. Paging didn't help. Maybe she was off showing him the Tomb of the Virgin. I left a message for each that Harry was okay and Superintendent Alboker had the details. If Alboker had told the embassy, Spaulding might already have given them the news. Putting down the phone, I asked Harry, "Do Morgenstern and Ozick know the real terms of the deal?"

I was betting I knew the answer. Harry was the only one of the three who had built a villa in Shomrim Tsion.

He laced his fingers together and stared at the ceiling. "They didn't, chum, until you gave Warren the business plan. Now I guess I'm in a little trouble."

TWELVE

The police kept Harry talking for two hours, after which he got testy and told them it was piss-off time. He gave them the whole shebang, he said, except for the details on Agritech, his suspicions about Dov Levy, and his doubts about Esther. Just the little stuff. "They think I'm holding back," he complained as we climbed the stairway to Agritech's office. He had talked to Karen by telephone, promised he would be at the hotel by six. He had promised Warren Morgenstern a full report as soon as the police cut him loose.

It was five past six when Esther opened the door to the office suite and let us in. "I don't understand what is going on," she said, stepping back.

I glanced around the office. Sometime in the last thirty-six hours it had been stripped almost to the walls. As Harry saw the barren rooms, his face darkened and he glanced at Esther. "What the hell do you know about this?" he said.

"I—nothing! It was all right yesterday morning." She

didn't like his tone, and her eyes were hurt. "This afternoon when I arrived—everything is gone!"

"Where's that Russian nitwit of yours?"

She shrugged. "Not here."

The place had been cleaned out with remarkable thoroughness on the one hand, but on the other the movers had been selective. Left behind were two battered desks, two swivel chairs, a tubular computer stand, and several file cabinet housings. Gone were the file drawers and desk drawers, the computer stations and hard drives, telephones, and all the boxes of documents that I'd seen Dov Levy's helper lugging around the suite. Without looking further, I knew that all the documentary evidence of Agritech's existence—all the corporate records, invoices, checks, bank books, and maybe even stationery—had been hauled away. Even for a company of Agritech's tiny size, the removal would have taken hours.

"I suppose the police could have done it," Harry said.

Checking the possibility was easy. Esther went downstairs to the hot dog and sauerkraut shop and started a vague conversation about the mess the moving people had left. It couldn't have taken them so long they couldn't straighten up after themselves. They'd probably blocked the shop with their trucks. It would have been fine with her if the owner, who was also Agritech's landlord, had called the police. The shopkeeper liked having a pretty woman to talk to. He was an aging Yemenite and excessively courteous. He said it was a pity when men made messes for fine women. He did not mention uniformed men taking part, even after she repeated that the police *certainly* could have been called. But no, they had not blocked the shop entrance, and in any case her man Yura had been most considerate as he supervised. His three or four helpers had been quite efficient. It had taken little more than an hour. And the shopkeeper hoped the filing warehouse would be convenient for Esther, who was welcome to visit his shop more often. But how was the company to continue without Dov? It was such a tragedy for a young man's family. And did she think the police had any clues? The officers who had come around that morning to talk to him hadn't seemed to know very much. The police had spent an hour upstairs, using his master key, but hadn't called in laboratory people. When, Esther asked, had the movers arrived? The shopkeeper told her it was soon after the police departed.

"Either they conned your stupid Russian, or he was helping them," Harry said.

"He's not *my* Russian," Esther said.

Harry stared at a file cabinet's empty sockets. "Warren won't like this," he said.

Esther *turned over* the Fiesta's keys to me. She didn't want to be on hand for Harry and Karen Brickman's reunion. I called from the Yemenite's shop and told Karen we were on our way.

She stayed in her room while Warren met Harry in the lobby. His lined gray face seemed to drop five years at the sight of his partner, whom he embraced with crushing fervor until Harry squealed. Warren Morgenstern held Harry at arm's length, eyes shiny. "When God brings the dead back," he said, "it's enough to make me religious."

Harry looked embarrassed.

"Don't worry, my friend," Warren said, "it will wear off. Now go upstairs. Your wife is waiting. We'll talk later. You look like hell, but she will never notice."

Obediently, Harry started for the elevator. He was almost there when he came back sheepishly and asked his partner for the room number.

Morgenstern watched him go, and the age came back on him. He was the oldest of the three principals of Morgenstern Ozick, a few years past sixty, I guessed. Of his life outside the context of Harry Brickman, I knew nothing. If he had a family—a shrewish wife and drug-addicted offspring, or some happier kind—Harry had never mentioned them. But there had never been a conversation between us leading in that direction. I knew about Harry's current wife from offhand complaints that pepper even some devoted husbands' conversation. I knew about Little Aaron because his father left work early on evenings when there was a pony league baseball game. I knew about the horrors of his divorce ten years ago because he warned me never to marry anything female, in terms worthy of Gideon Larkis. It went with the territory. I knew he hadn't talked to either of his grown sons in years because he lumped family disaffections, along with client lawsuits, into the soup of "the human predicament," which a reasonable man learned to accept, the bitter with the sweet. I knew that Ben Ozick was a confirmed bachelor because Harry claimed him as a convert. Warren Morgenstern was older and presumably beyond Harry's influence on matters of family, fidelity, or the ingredients of the human predicament.

He clapped me on the shoulder. "They don't need us. What do you say to a drink?"

The terrace was three-quarters deserted. We got a table, ordered drinks. "This has been a strain," he said. "I'm sorry we gave Harry his lead on this idea of starting companies over here. To feel strongly about Israel is one thing. If a Jew doesn't hate himself, he feels strongly about Israel. But to put your own money and your clients' money here where you can't watch it closely!" He shrugged. "I never said it in these words to Harry, but I should have: It's *stupid!*"

Our drinks came and he raised his. *"L'chaim."*

I lifted my beer and drank. *L'chaim.* To life. He sounded more disappointed in his own judgment than furious at Harry. The response was mild if he'd read Dov Levy's blue notebook and understood its significance. Harry hadn't mentioned the notebook to him or the condition of Agritech's office.

"Tell me what happened," Warren said. "Harry was taken by Arabs, he escaped—what was it all about?"

"He doesn't think they were Arabs," I said. I wondered if the police had found a body at the abandoned settlement. I told him as much as I could without closing off Harry's options. That left Esther Sennesh as a helpful driver. It didn't allow anything about Harry's suspicion of Dov Levy. To my own ear, the story came out halting and fragmented. He would have been entitled to doubt its completeness. I hoped he concluded I didn't know or understand any more than he did.

"Have the police made any progress on Levy?" I asked.

"Not that they've chosen to share with me. I knew their questions about you were nonsense. If you were driving with him, I told them, it didn't mean you were murdering him. When that girl came to your defense, they dropped it. What does that tell you?"

I shook my head.

"That their tip was anonymous. Now this Alboker or whoever's got the ball is probably wondering about the tipper."

"Not a bad idea," I said. I could think of other possibilities. One was that Alboker wasn't above kidding a guy with made-up information, to see what response he got. Nobody in the police had been specific about when I'd been seen with Levy, or where. If Alboker had invented the tip, he wouldn't have lost interest in me. Except that Esther had vouched for my whereabouts and good conduct.

Once the police got wind that Agritech's finances weren't kosher, Esther's word wouldn't be worth much. Even if Harry swore he'd been bound and gagged in the desert, the police would think he'd had a good reason to even up with Dov Levy. It wouldn't be a stretch for them to suspect his Irish friend from New York had helped. Or his partner. Or even, stretching just a little, his wife. Or, not stretching much at all, Esther. Warren Morgenstern had been in town less than twenty-four hours when Levy was killed. Mrs. Brickman the same. Esther had even better opportunity, and if the police began suspecting both of us, our mutual alibi would be useless. It occurred to me that the more the police believed Harry's story of being kidnapped, the stronger his motive appeared for murdering Dov. All you had to assume was that Dov had arranged the kidnapping to cover his financial shenanigans.

It would be only fair to give Warren a hint that things could get sticky. I couldn't think of how to put a toe into the subject without getting in waist deep. It was up to Harry to tell his partner what was going on.

I didn't want to be around for that conversation.

Warren looked across the treetops to the walls of the Old City. The early evening sun was coming at a low angle, bathing the stones in colors I supposed a painter would have liked. Whatever the city's associations for Warren or Harry, it seemed an unromantic place to me. The McCarrys hadn't raised religious boys. The city's Christian shrines were as emotionally meaningless to me as the Jewish and Muslim sites. It was just an old walled city, not very attractive in its own right, where centuries of blood had been spilled by people convinced of things they couldn't see or prove. An argument, it seemed to me, against reading certain books. You might get caught up in the debate.

Esther's politics seemed easier to endorse. She was determined to continue living. If that meant carrying an Uzi on the floor of her car, so be it. If she referred to regions by biblical names, it was because she knew them by those names. If she had a religion, it was a faith of the flesh.

My mind was drifting, and I missed Warren Morgenstern's next words. His long face stretched into a tired smile. "I was saying this is a place that makes people crazy. People come to Jerusalem and decide they're King David, or Jesus. The psychiatric hospitals get them every week."

"It happens in New York as well," I said, "but nobody locks them up."

He chuckled, more from duty than amusement. "I would say there is a difference. The crazy people in New York would be crazy anywhere. There are crazy people in Chicago. The peculiar effect of Jerusalem is observed in psychiatric literature."

When he understood what Harry had been up to with Dov Levy, I wondered if he would dismiss his partner's fraud as a psychiatric aberration.

I *went upstairs,* showered, and settled down by the telephone in one of the hotel's terry cloth robes. It was early afternoon in New York. Magee & Temple was humming. Meg Sorkin was juggling calls and cut me off after assuring me the market wasn't doing much. I left it at that. The office felt unreal, part of someone else's life. Stock prices seemed as meaningless as day-old sports scores. I'd been due to arrive in New York more than twelve hours ago, and from Meg's complacent tone, nobody seemed worried that I hadn't appeared.

I was wrong. I'd turned off the light and collapsed into bed when the phone rang. The voice on the other end was pretty, feminine, well-educated, all things that were true of the woman it went with. "Donald? *Donald?* Oh, darling! We've been so worried about you. I expected you this morning. Then the airline said you weren't aboard."

"There was a small mix-up," I said.

Stacy Kimball didn't ask what sort of mix-up, since the reason for my nonarrival didn't affect her, only the consequence. But her indifference was innocent. "Will you be here tomorrow?"

Given the twelve or thirteen hour flight time, that would have required I be on this evening's plane. Superintendent Alboker hadn't said anything this afternoon about my leaving. I no longer was officially a suspect in Dov Levy's death. I wasn't being detained. He'd given me my passport after Esther intervened. Unless he got another anonymous call, I could probably leave tomorrow. "There's been a little problem," I said, "and it may keep me here a couple of days."

"Oh . . ." She sounded disappointed, almost concerned. "Is the problem serious? Do you think Daddy could help?"

The last thing I wanted was Charlie Kimball pulling strings on my behalf. Assuming it would be on my behalf. I said quickly, "The investment isn't looking too good."

"Oh." Dreariness set in. She wouldn't say she didn't care about investment problems, but she couldn't keep the truth out of her voice. Buying and selling stocks, making investments for other people, just didn't fit her definition of serious work. The Kimball family's level of prosperity owed to its control of Tracer Minerals. At some level, Stacy, her sister, and their father all viewed anything not closely linked to Tracer as being at least partly frivolous.

I echoed her "Oh" and added, "I'll be back before you know it. Harry and I will get things straightened out."

"I hope so." There was a hint in her voice that she might not put up with my neglect forever. "Some of your Wall Street friends aren't the best quality. You can disagree, but I wouldn't do business with anyone like Harry Brickman." She'd met him once, found him vulgar, not to mention Jewish.

"One of these days, you're going to wake up to what coarse fellows the Irish are," I said, "and then it will be all over."

"I can tolerate one crass person in my life. His name just isn't Brickman." And never would be, or anything remotely similar, I knew, and wondered if she understood it as well in its unvarnished form. It wouldn't make her less important to me. It might make me ask myself why she wasn't.

She had inherited her attitudes, I told myself, not chosen them. It made a difference.

We said good night—I did, Stacy said she was going to lunch—and I went to sleep.

Harry woke me up long before I was ready by banging on the door. It was 8:30 A.M., and the room was gray. Alboker's come to arrest me, I thought, or Spaulding to check my loyalty. I put on the robe, opened the door, and Harry grinned. "You feel like joining Karen and me for breakfast? Ten minutes in the café?"

"All right."

He looked past me into the room, and I realized he was looking for Esther. "See you downstairs," he said.

It took me closer to fifteen minutes. The morning was bleak and cold. Rain had wet the carpet where I had left the casement windows ajar. The tiny balcony was slick and reflected thick gray clouds. Across the gorge, small cars raced uphill to the Old City as if the road were dry. I shaved and pulled on clothes.

Downstairs, the Gan Dan Café was chilly and full of rainy light. Warren Morgenstern was at the table with the Brick-

159

mans when I arrived. He was wearing a gray flannel suit and a two-toned shirt with a gray and black necktie. It suited the day. He was listening as Harry and Karen talked, his hand across the top of a coffee cup as if warding off a nonexistent waiter. Karen Brickman looked tired but cheerful. Harry hadn't told her he'd gone native. As I pulled back a chair, he looked up, excited. "Have you heard—the police are looking for Yura."

"Levy's Russian?" I hadn't heard, couldn't imagine how he thought I might have. "What for?"

"Cleaning out Agritech," Harry said without a glance at his partner. "Hell of a thing—anything that could be sold is gone."

That wasn't how I remembered the scene. The skeletons of file cabinets and desks had been left behind. Things that could be sold but wouldn't yield information. But if Harry was peddling that line, Warren seemed willing to buy.

The older man shook his head. "It's a sad thing. Are these immigrants in a bad way?"

"Not as long as there are things to steal," Harry said.

Karen Brickman gave her husband a dark stare. "They aren't all thieves. The little newsletter the hotel gives you says there are a number of Russian emigrés on staff. They wouldn't keep them if they stole from guests."

"I didn't say *all* of them."

"You certainly implied it."

A man had come to the table unobserved. He said, "Mrs. Brickman is correct. There are many honest immigrants from the former Soviet Union." I looked over my shoulder and saw Alboker's narrow, handsome face. He was wearing an open-necked white shirt, dark trousers, black loafers and carried his little portfolio. I wondered if we were in for more mug shots. "Sorry to interrupt. But Mr. Brickman also is correct in his insinuation. Criminality among the Russian immigrants is a problem. Prostitution among the women is epidemic, and we are seeing more extortion. They are highly organized, like the Mafia. I wanted to let you know that we have a prime suspect in Mr. Levy's murder, and as I suspected, the motive was simplicity itself: as one would expect, money. Mr. Levy was observed before noon in the company of a large, heavily bearded man who very closely fits the description of Yura Geller. This sighting is reliable, unlike the report implicating Mr. McCarry."

"He killed Levy?" It was Harry, round-mouthed.

"Miss Sennesh informed me that a certain amount of cash normally was kept on hand for office expenses. Not a large sum—at most, one thousand new shekels—but that might seem a great deal to Yura Geller. Miss Sennesh informed me that this money, along with much else, was missing from the office yesterday afternoon."

Karen Brickman met the policeman's eye and asked, "Would a thousand shekels seem like a lot of money to Miss Sennesh?"

"It is possible. She is not a suspect, however. At the time of the killing, she vouches for Mr. McCarry's whereabouts and, by extension, for her own." He didn't ask if I wanted to dispute that.

Harry was giving his wife a long, bothered stare. He had to be wondering why she zeroed in on Esther Sennesh.

"Have the police apprehended this Geller person?" said Warren.

"We will do so. He cannot leave Israel."

"But if he's got friends," Harry said.

"We will find him. I must be on my way."

Warren watched him leave and then said to Harry, "For a thousand shekels, the man has done a lot of damage. Am I right in thinking that without Levy, Agritech will be unable to continue? So then, will we lose all the investment?"

Harry was watching Morgenstern with the look of a man who had grown impatient waiting to be accused. "We shouldn't have a loss at all, Warren," he said.

"There were reserves?"

"Not exactly, but we have an insurance policy."

"That's good news, and it reminds me. Here, take this. I never read them because they are not worth the paper and ink, and after I heard about Levy I knew this one was doubly useless." Digging into a battered leather briefcase, he came up with a blue-bound notebook and chipped it across the table to Harry. "Give the damned company a quick burial. All right, Harry?"

Harry nodded. "Whatever happens, we're out of it, and out whole."

"That's all I ask. We can take crazy risks at home. In fact, while you and I are getting religion over here, Ben is probably wrecking our portfolios. I should call him right now."

"It's three in the morning in New York."

"Even better." He made getting up motions. "You'll excuse me?"

Harry watched him go. His expression to anyone else might have been meaningless. To me, it was a giddy mixture of relief and self-satisfaction. He had gotten away with it. Warren hadn't read Levy's business plan with its incriminating mention of a nine percent guarantee. He hadn't pressed for details on the insurance policy. All Harry had to do was put in his claim to the Ministry of Economic Development, return the capital plus a small profit to his partners, and he was home free. He dug into breakfast with gusto, chattering to his wife about a little sight-seeing—maybe he would find he was home free with her, too—and all but winking at me. In the end, his good cheer said, everything works out right.

I thought for a while and said, "You know that insurance

you mentioned? I hope the papers documenting the terms weren't with the stuff Yura stole."

He coughed a shred of smoked salmon across the table. His face was blank, almost white. Karen Brickman grabbed his hand. "Darling—"

"I'm okay." He wheezed. He drank water, hiccuped, gave her a shaky smile, and me a look of pale terror.

His *excuse for* ducking out after breakfast was setting up a conference call with Agritech's field personnel to discuss the future of the company. I went with him. In Agritech's Fiesta, as its wipers clicked at half-hearted spatters, he groaned. "I don't know if they even *have* conference calls in Israel."

"Probably not to Ethiopia."

"You're helpful as hell."

"If she finds out, you can kid her about that, too."

He ignored the jibe. "Stop here a minute."

We were on Jaffa, headed away from the Old City. I pulled to the curb and he dashed across the sidewalk and back fifty paces to a wall telephone. In a minute he came back.

"Esther's got the goddamn key to the office. She'll meet us."

"The hot dog shop's owner could let us in," I said.

"No matter. She's on her way now."

I parked in the neighborhood and we walked down the pedestrian mall. The shop's owner was on an errand, according to the sign he'd posted. We waited in the stairway, watching the few passersby, and Harry said, "You know the main problem here? It isn't the immigrants. It isn't the Intifada. Business sucks. That's the problem."

"You're down on things."

163

"No, I'm a natural optimist. You know that. Who would be stupid enough to think he could get away with my scam if he wasn't an optimist?" He held Dov Levy's notebook under an arm. I was a little surprised he hadn't torn out pages and scattered them as we drove. "It's just—can you imagine teaching Jews how *not* to do business? How not to make money? That's what the schmucks running this show have done. That deal with the Development Ministry— have you ever heard of anything so fucking dumb? If we go broke, that fat pig in the Ministry says, 'That's okay, the State of Israel will pick up the tab.' "

"Who's the pig?"

"Yigal Martin, deputy minister, assistant minister—I've forgotten. Just another public sector operator. They're falling all over each other."

Esther came through the rain, wearing her inevitable denims, along with a white shirt, a camouflage jacket across her shoulders, a bright scarf on her head. She ran past us without greeting and up the stairs, unlocked the suite, and switched on the lights. She cast around. No drawers were left, but there were places in the drawer wells to check. "I don't know where Dov had our contract with the Ministry," she mumbled.

"Sweetheart, you were in charge of paperwork," Harry said.

"I know where *I* kept it, with our other most important documents. We have contracts for the equipment, agreements with employees. Dov had the Ministry contract out recently, and I don't know if it got put back." She stood with a hand on the cross bar of an empty file slot. "If it did, it's gone. It shouldn't matter. Yigal Martin will have copies."

Harry rubbed his forehead. "Can you believe I invest in a

company that doesn't have off-premises backups? Worse—I never demanded it."

"I will call the Ministry," Esther said. "It will all be well."

"No it won't. We don't have records of expenditures, receipts, investors, or even who's working for us. We don't even have a copy of Agritech's charter! The Ministry isn't going to write a check because we say so."

"Much of the information can be obtained—bank records, certainly, though it will take time."

"I don't have much time. If I can't reimburse our investors, my partners are going to start wondering why. So far Warren believes me. A week from now, he won't, quite as much. He'll say to himself 'What kind of insurance can my friend Harry have? Business failure insurance? Who has heard of such a thing? A life insurance policy on Mr. Levy? For such a sum?' And he'll want our auditors to talk to me and see some kind of paper to prove I haven't been diddling everybody."

"Perhaps the police will find Yura."

"They hadn't as of forty minutes ago."

"When they do—"

"When they do," I interrupted her, "it will probably be in another orange grove, don't you think?"

"Who would do that?"

"Whoever he's working with. Or whoever he and Levy were working with."

"Dov wouldn't have—"

"It had to be someone. Money didn't drain out of Agritech on its own. I assume you didn't write the checks. Did Levy or did you?"

"Dov wrote the checks," she said, obviously angry. "But Dov would not steal from this company."

"Then it was you."

She took two steps toward me, brushed off Harry's restraining hand. I didn't know what she had learned during her national service about personal combat, but her intent was clearly to give me a demonstration.

I said quickly, "If it wasn't you or Levy, we have a problem."

A little of the murder left her eyes. Turning her back, she folded her arms and kicked a trash can into a filing cabinet. As both objects were metal, the crash was resoundingly satisfactory.

"Who else could have tapped into the company?" I said.

"I do not know." She wouldn't turn around to look at me.

Harry butted in. "I vote for Dov. I liked him but—"

"You *liked* him and you say that?" she exploded.

"McCarry's right, honey. I didn't sign the company's checks. You didn't. That leaves Dov. If we just had the invoices, the vendor receipts, the cancelled checks, we could make sense of it. We could at least figure out how much is missing."

"I will talk to the bank," Esther said. "It is Friday, so I had better do it before they close for Shabbat."

Harry nodded. "And McCarry and I will go see my friend Yigal Martin."

We locked the door and headed downstairs. The rain was on again, spattering the hot dog man's outdoor chairs and tables. Harry slapped my shoulder. "Which of us gets wet to bring the car around?" The friendly pat was supposed to convince me to volunteer. Telling myself it couldn't hurt to make him feel good, I said I would go. A half block ahead, I spotted one reason Superintendent Alboker wasn't making progress on Yura. He had his stakeout team in their white Mercedes keeping an eye on us. The car sat in front of a bakery, wheels straddling a stream of rainwater, wipers clicking, windows fogged, exhaust sputtering. Not the subtlest surveillance, but if I hadn't spotted them a few nights ago at the Moriah, I wouldn't have paid attention. The car would have been just another shopkeeper nudging into the empty pedestrian mall to make loading easier.

I hurried, though after the first thirty seconds I was as wet as anyone could get. We'd parked only a block away. It took me a couple of minutes to run the distance, get settled in the car, start the engine. Less than a minute more to reach the street feeding into Ben Yehuda, bump over the low curb onto the pedestrian mall, and turn the corner.

Not long at all, but the shooting was over.

Harry and Esther were down on the sidewalk, and if there was blood it was being washed away. Two men wearing olive army uniforms were standing halfway out of their car, each in an almost identical pose as though in mirror image, one foot on the pavement, one in the car, a weapon pointed at the bodies, one with a direct field of fire, the other aiming across the car roof. The car was canted toward the hot dog shop. As the man on the farther side started around the back of his car, intent clear, I pressed the accelerator. Neither of them heard the engine for what seemed like a long time. It was the man closest to me who looked around, bearded face opening in surprise, and brought his machine gun around. He sprayed the windshield, but I was flat across the seat by then and didn't hear the shots or feel the glass explode. I didn't hear the cars strike. The impact of the dashboard slammed me lengthwise from hip to shoulder. The gear knob jabbed my belly as I flew over it.

Pulling myself out of the footwell seemed urgent. I pushed and got an arm onto a seat. Holding the dashboard with one hand, I wriggled backward until the door blocked me. I reached behind me and pulled on the latch.

The door opened and I backed out.

The nearer man was on the Fiesta's hood and ended just

below the waist. I looked for his partner. It was only from the other side of the car that I saw where he had been hurled by the impact. He lay against a concrete planter filled with yellow petunias, an arm twisted behind him, face convulsed in pain.

When I got to Harry and Esther, sprawled at the doorway, I took one look. They were both dead. There was blood in the doorway that the rain hadn't reached. There were white shards and tufts of hair on the pavement. Harry was slumped against the door frame. His meaty left forearm rose and fell back. The hand trembled. I watched, mesmerized. The top quarter of his head was gone, and his half-open right eye was sightless. His arm moved again. I knelt and lifted it gently. Esther looked up at me, and a small hand kept pushing at the empty air. There were two large red patches on her shirt. She looked at me without comprehension.

The police arrived before she died. The ambulance came after. When she closed her eyes without recognizing me, I sat and held the hand that had been pushing against Harry. From their positions it looked as though he might have thrown himself in front of her. I hoped there had been time for heroism. She didn't ask about him. She said a few things I couldn't understand. A young policeman hovering over her responded in Hebrew. "She asks for a prayer," he said. He made no attempt to render first aid. Her chest was blowing pink froth. The flow of blood from her back was unstaunchable. Reading my mind, he said, "There is no reason to cause her pain."

He left but came back not much later. "Come on. There is someone alive over here."

The man was oval-faced with deep blue eyes and thin black hair. A shattered arm was cradled in his lap as he sat against the planter. He ignored a policeman who tried talk-

168

ing to him in Hebrew. He wore no expression that I could read.

I told the young officer who seemed to be in charge that Superintendent Alboker would want to be informed. When Alboker arrived, I told him everything I knew. My suggestion that the shooters might be Russian proved to be no revelation. "You are right, of course."

We sat in the back of a small police car. Alboker sprang out at the sound of gunfire.

I followed and saw the prisoner sprawled at the base of the planter. He had waited for the right moment, when only one policeman was guarding him. He had produced a knife from among the petunias and slashed the leg of the policeman, who responded with an Uzi burst that was instantly fatal. The description of events was Alboker's. If it worked for him, it worked for me.

THIRTEEN

Harry Brickman had made a will declaring he wanted to be buried in Israel. Spaulding turned Karen Brickman over to someone at the embassy who specialized in grieving relatives. Warren Morgenstern stuck close to her. I found myself an extra wheel and went back to the hotel.

She wouldn't come visiting today.

The morning and half the afternoon had worn away. I felt an almost uncontrollable urge to lift the phone and talk to someone in New York, almost anyone I knew, and hope they would go on at length about nothing. If Timmy Upham had a stock idea, if Isaiah Stern had a long obscene joke, if Meg Sorkin had office gossip, if Max Oberfeld wanted to tell me where he had moved my desk, if Stacy Kimball could think of steps to improve me, if her father wanted to compare forebears, I would listen gratefully as long as any of them wanted to talk. They would keep my ear jammed with noise, my attention jammed with details, just as if the room were full of people. And one of them would certainly ask how things were going with me, and then I could let it out and tell them. I would try to keep my voice steady, and if it broke I would blame a cold. There was no one I could call and tell the whole truth, and the absence of such a person made me feel as hollow as the room. I was one of those glib, clever people who needed nothing, to whom nothing mattered, and, in perfect symmetry, who had nothing that mattered. The insight was grim and unwelcome.

It made for a long afternoon.

When I could, I went downstairs. The rain had let up in teasing intermissions. The actor and his blonde were cutting up for their friends on the terrace. They weren't quite ridiculing each other but were getting close enough to feel the sharpness of the edge. I resisted an urge to go over and tell them why they shouldn't do that.

It would be useless advice. Some knowledge existed only in post hoc form.

Besides, the blonde might be a thoroughgoing pain in the neck. A shopping list in one hand, a spouse improvement list in the other, a long cool pedigree in place of the inner furnace.

Or she might be stealing from you before your eyes.

Which brought me back to Esther. If Agritech had gone through more money than it could have spent legitimately, how had the excess left the firm? The particulars didn't matter, because there were dozens of ways it could have been done: padded invoices with kickbacks; vendors created from the whole cloth—that way you could funnel money to yourself directly, without a middle man. The "how" I was looking for came from a smaller set of possibilities. You could refine it a little, but basically somebody within Agritech had to be directing money to the outside. Drawing out cash invited questions. Looting usually was done by check. The loyal corporate treasurer every month writes

171

ninety-nine checks to real suppliers and employees and one check to his or her own little shell company that produces the most convincing invoices. Medium-sized companies set up all sorts of safeguards, purchasing orders, frequent spot checks of inventory against invoices, division of responsibilities between the keeper of the books and the writer of checks. Simple stuff, routine. The dedicated thief circumvents these safeguards. At small companies, where resources for security are limited and the longtime employee is regarded as family, the owner finds out the truth only when his loyal check writer doesn't turn up for work on Monday and on Tuesday his payroll bounces.

Very good, McCarry. You have a couple of friends who are accountants. They bemoan the horror stories and laugh at them at the same time. *"For nine years, naughty Marietta was spending every Saturday and Sunday in Atlantic City, and every Monday the boss asked if she'd had a nice weekend and let it go at 'Yes, Mr. Fester, I played bridge and baby-sat my sister's kids.' Nine years, and no one ever saw her on a weekend and nobody ever wondered."*

I knew the stories all right. It was always a person writing checks.

Always.

Which meant Dov or Esther.

Or both. There was nobody else. The other employees were abroad. The other director, Harry, didn't have the checkbook. The computer programmer from Moscow, Yura Geller, didn't program computers and didn't write checks. He had helped strip the office and had disappeared. The gunmen were Russian emigrés, for all I knew doctors and scientists back home but more likely criminals there, too. The man Harry coldcocked in the desert hadn't been Arab, but he could have been Russian.

Which, I thought, would eliminate coincidence and might also absolve Dov and Esther.

Was it farfetched to think Yura had tapped Agritech's accounts by computer? I could ask Alboker if the emigré gangs had done similar jobs. We might both have an answer. To Alboker, the answer might even matter.

Finishing a drink I didn't want, I called the police headquarters and ran my idea past Alboker. It was possible, he said. If I thought of anything more, I could call.

"Did you find any sign of them in the desert?"

"We found evidence that someone had been living there. Nothing so far that is useful. No body of a bearded man. If Brickman had notified us sooner, it might have been otherwise."

"What about the shooters?"

"Members of a local emigré gang, as I surmised. They were professional criminals. Israel does not have many such, but we are not immune." He added as an afterthought, "If they are among the group that held your friend, the motive may have been ransom."

When I told him I wanted to return to New York, he said I was free to go. His tone was abstracted, as if the case were largely closed. If they found Yura Geller, I supposed it would be.

El Al didn't fly on the Sabbath but had a flight the following evening. I booked a seat and watched the change that came over the New City as evening approached. The street emptied of cars. Pedestrians appeared on the broad, tree-lined sidewalks heading in the direction of the Old City. The hotel quieted for a while and then became busier. I rang Warren's room and suggested we meet downstairs. I owed him as much of the truth about Harry as I knew, assuming Alboker hadn't filled him in. He came down ten minutes after I got there. Service had stopped on the terrace, but we sat at a table still beaded with water. The sky looked like it might manage another bout of rain. Warren was dressed no more somberly than he had been at breakfast: a dark flannel suit; a white-on-white shirt; a gray necktie. His face sagged in long pouches. The underside of his eyes looked raw. He slumped onto a chair, hands tucked into his jacket pockets. "She is devastated, just destroyed," he rasped.

"You don't look great yourself."

"Me? I would like to have one chance to tell Brickman what a putz he was. What a bastard. In our business, you don't fuck around with clients' money." He shook his head. "Ben and I will have to make everyone whole out of our own pockets—and out of the deceased bastard's. Karen doesn't know that part yet. Someone else made her a widow. I am going to make her a poor widow."

So Alboker had told him. "It may not be that bad," I said. "There was an agreement with the Ministry of Economic Development guaranteeing nine percent."

"Was there. Who told you?"

"Harry."

"I spent ninety minutes with Yigal Martin. The Ministry does not underwrite fraud, he explained. Agritech's operating losses—those we might talk about later, assuming they can be documented. But money extracted from the firm under false pretenses, or stolen outright—for that, the Ministry disclaims responsibility. I must understand. It is the responsibility of the investors to act prudently and in good faith."

I told him what Alboker had told me about emigré gangsters.

"It makes sense, I suppose," he said wearily. "Well, I've

174

got to make a phone call to New York. Ben hasn't heard any of this day's news. Will you be here for the services?"

"When are they?"

"Sunday. It's customary to bury the dead as soon as possible, but nothing happens here on Shabbat."

"My plane's tomorrow evening."

He shrugged. "No matter, my friend. Funerals are for relatives and people who never liked the guy."

Through the glass doors, I could see people milling beyond the lounge. "What's going on in the hotel?"

"Shabbat dinner, served by Christian Arabs." Seeing my expression, he said, "Observant Jews do no work between sundown Friday and sundown Saturday. Some take it very seriously." Something in his tone said it was a nice custom but not for him. He crossed his legs and looked into the lighted hall. "Very seriously. The Orthodox live near their synagogue so they can walk to shul because they cannot drive. If you use the elevator, you will find that it is programmed now to stop at every floor; that is so that no buttons need be pushed. The lights that will be needed were turned on before sunset and will remain on until tomorrow evening. Stoves cannot be lighted." Another shrug. "Fortunately, many Jews are not religious, so the country goes on."

"They get by, you mean."

"And that's nothing to belittle, getting by." He uncrossed his legs, got up, smoothed his suit. "About Harry. I saw the body. He couldn't have suffered."

"I wouldn't think so."

"You got there right after. Did he say anything?"

"He was dead."

"People sometimes, even with horrible wounds. . . . It would be nice for Karen to hear he spoke her name."

The part of Harry's brain that knew her might have been

on the pavement. Did fragments lie remembering? Without identity—not *This is Harry thinking* but a chatter of stored bits discharging like random sparks, *Karen . . . teaspoon . . . Wednesday . . . Succoth . . .*—for just a few seconds?

"Tell her he spoke her name. I seem to remember it that way."

"Thank you. What about the Israeli girl?"

He wasn't asking whether she'd had Karen Brickman in her last thoughts. I said, "She didn't suffer either." I didn't know. Maybe she hadn't.

"When I get back to New York, would you mind getting together?" He asked tentatively, like an old man afraid of imposing. An evening devoted to remembering Harry's finer moments would indeed be imposing. I told him I would be happy to. He nodded at the empty air. "Come on inside. You don't want to sit out here alone."

I wouldn't have minded. I went inside with him, then said I was going for a walk. I got as far as Yemin Moshe, Montefiore's windmill, without letting Harry or Esther's face creep into my mind. In the narrow streets filled with the fragrance of cascading flowers, the girl became impossible to hold at bay. A Persian queen, an easy drunk, a foolish mistress, an impermanent thing.

All flesh is grass, all beauty. . . . I couldn't remember the rest, didn't think I wanted to. It was bad news, whether from a poet on a bender or a prophet with a bee in his bonnet, someone who understood more than I did.

I *paid a* call on Karen Brickman the next morning. She had a large suite on an upper floor with paneled walls and long mirrors. She wanted to talk about Harry, his silly excesses, his foolish impulses. The house in Shomrim Tsion would be sold. She hadn't seen it but understood I had and she wondered what I thought of it. I said it was a nice house by Israeli standards in a rather religious community. She shook her head. "Harry hadn't a religious bone in his body. I really don't understand. . . ."

I wondered if Warren had told her about people coming to Jerusalem and deciding they were Moses. It wasn't the worst news he had for her. If he had mentioned the firm's claim against Harry's estate, it didn't seem to be on her mind. I didn't know how much Harry had been worth. If Morgenstern Ozick had to recover a couple of million, it could leave a dent. He might have more than that in assets, but assets weren't cash.

She sat on a small striped sofa, a glass table between us laid with morning coffee, fruit, and cheese. She was wearing a gray dress and gold earrings, not quite funeral clothes but probably the closest she had packed.

"I'm sorry I won't be here for the funeral," I said.

"It will feel strange leaving Harry here, almost like he was never part of our lives. He'll be at the Mount of Olives. I gather there is more than one cemetery there. A woman from the embassy explained. She said she couldn't believe how many Jews who had lived their entire lives in the United States wanted to be buried in Israel."

Her small face was puzzled, and her eyes studied me as if expecting an explanation. I was back in my room and packing when I thought of one, flip but serviceable. Harry's reason could be pragmatic. All the good spots near the stock exchange were taken.

FOURTEEN

My *loft in* SoHo wasn't noticeably stale for a week's neglect. Mail had gathered downstairs. Nothing surfaced in the pile that at 6:30 on a Sunday morning seemed to demand attention. There was a postcard from Harry showing an artist's rendering of the old windmill at Yemin Moshe. He hadn't said much:

> I may indeed open a Jerusalem office.

Inspired by Esther?

Without unpacking, I crashed for six hours. I woke up feeling detached and distant from the other part of the world. Already the New City's streets were blurring, colors and smells fading, noises sailing into the holes memory opens for the fact which is no longer needed. In a day or two I wouldn't remember the color of the King David's carpets. A week later Dov Levy's face would lose its lumpy character. The lawns of the YMCA would become undifferentiated green, giving up their beds of flowers. Esther's voice would lose its definition and merge into generic young womanhood's softness. Her fragrance and touch would be memory instead of a reality that had just stepped out of the room for a moment. Finally, there would be not memory but memory of memory, formalized and fixed with all its vivid definition gone.

I took my time unpacking. Took my time on a melted cheese sandwich. Then I phoned Stacy and got her answering machine. I tried the house in Connecticut and got her father's answering machine. I left messages both places. Then I put on a gray suit and, for the first time in days, a necktie, and found a taxi headed downtown.

The lobby at Magee & Temple's headquarters is empty on weekends except for whatever part of the security staff happens to have gathered there. Today two women in burgundy uniforms were chatting across the console that held the building directory. At the lobby's north end, the financial quote boards suspended from the mezzanine were dark. They drew a crowd on weekdays. Trading went on in some instrument in some part of the world either quietly or hysterically even on a Sunday afternoon, but nobody came down to Wall Street to watch. I signed in and took the one elevator they had running up to eighteen. Magee & Temple doesn't do much in international markets, but a few people occupy certain desks every minute of every day. Traders for the firm's account keep watch for devaluations, political upheavals, central bank mischief—anything that might expose Magee & Temple to an avalanche of selling or a stampede of buying from its customers a few hours later. The traders might lay off some interest-rate risk in London, short dollars in Hong Kong, or buy a position in the Nikkei in Japan. None of that occurs on the eighteenth floor. Our suite was empty, silent, without even the submerged hum of air circulation. From late Friday afternoon until Monday

179

morning, on most floors the ventilation was shut down. If the last scent on Friday had been fear, it would linger like dust on everything until the air resumed flowing on Monday. I crossed the suite from the elevator and, smelling nothing in particular, concluded that Friday had been a boring day. No panic, no elation, just comfortable, profitable commerce.

My key still opened the door to my office, which I was happy to find undisturbed. Mad Max must have found another cubbyhole for Howard, or Howard had gotten a closer look at Magee & Temple's fast track for geniuses and had jumped over to Salomon Brothers. I turned up the illumination on the ADP and spent twenty minutes catching up on prices. Meg had kept me half-posted by telephone. None of the stocks in which we had big positions had done anything ugly, but there were a couple of dozen names spread through clients' portfolios, and I had to go through the entire roster. Most hadn't moved more than a point. Two had swung several points—both up, which was heartening but also cause for a little uneasiness because I hadn't a clue what people saw in them that hadn't been there a week ago. I jumped from screen to screen, calling up news items when it looked as though something might have been announced. All in all, I had picked a boring week to be away. Timmy Upham or Isaiah Stern had put through only a handful of trades for my clients, most of whom seemed content not to call us if we weren't calling them.

The phone messages were in a little box on Meg's desk. A few customers had wanted their weekly quota of handholding. I went through them with the patience of a man determined to keep himself distracted. The idiot calls went on the bottom: clients who believed brokers had to be given a hard time or they got out of line; touts who called the moment they were done buying and invited me to join the daisy chain. The next category consisted of people I didn't want to talk to but couldn't ignore: the back office at Magee & Temple; clients who needed something done, an old tax shelter looked at, a reminder sent to our people that cash balances earn interest. Then came anything that promised to be interesting, which included a few fellow brokers who occasionally shared a good idea. When I was done sorting I had one message left over that I couldn't put in a category.

Gideon Larkis. The date was three days ago, the number a midtown Manhattan exchange. By way of a message there was just Meg's recognizable *pls cl.*

My memory dredged up an image of the sallow-faced, black-haired man who was both lawyer and sometime client to Morgenstern Ozick. Gideon Larkis, who wanted to divorce a third or fourth wife while keeping the fruits of his past labors. I stared at the memo. After I'd turned down his attempt to create fraudulent losses, Larkis had tried leaving the country with a suitcase full of cash. Trying to get it out of his wife's reach, Harry said. If he'd told me her name, I couldn't remember. I put Larkis's message on the bottom of the stack. I had enough problems with clients who were more or less honest. The kind who thought in large amounts of cash and sham losses could work with my colleagues. Preferably with Mad Max himself. If a deal went sour and Gideon Larkis got mad at somebody, Max was my first choice.

It took me another hour to shovel through the week's accumulated paperwork to the point where I thought I could face Monday morning. We'd had a couple of dozen limit orders in place that had been hit, selling clients out of positions, covering one short sale, buying pieces of one stock that had looked especially cheap. Viscount Industries had only gained a half point on the week, and I worried it might be running out of steam. It confronted me with one of the moral dilemmas of the stock brokering business. To stay with the stock of a good company for years, as the business grew and the share value expanded—that was one option. The other was to take a profit before it got away and invest the client's money in something new. It's a dilemma because a broker earns no commission by sitting still but takes in two commissions by selling one thing and buying another.

A dilemma also because it is easier to make one good decision than it is to make two good ones in a row.

I folded the tent. Viscount Industries could wait for tomorrow. The fate of young Howard, young Howard whose nose steered him to an endless succession of good investments, could also wait. Whether my desk stayed on the eighteenth floor or got consigned to a closet on the tenth, or got put into storage after its occupant found employment at another firm, could wait. My priority list was short. I wanted to see Stacy's bright hair and forget Esther Sennesh's dark braid. I wanted to have a drink with a client who didn't own Israeli companies. I wanted to forget my friend Harry, who hadn't been that much of a friend after all.

And I wanted to talk to Charlie Kimball. For once I could use his talent at string-pulling. I wanted to know how the Israelis handled things from here.

I folded forward, put my face on the desk, fought off the images of Ben Yehuda Street, and then gave into them.

Stacy answered her phone, cried out, "I was *wondering* when you were getting back!" The tone was just right: not chiding; "wondering" could have been "worrying" because I hadn't arrived, or "hoping" that I would arrive soon.

"I was wondering, too," I said.

"You sound exhausted. Are you too tired for dinner?"

"No. In fact, the prospect positively invigorates me."

"That sounds promising."

"Don't expect too much vigor. Jet lag, you know. Do you know where your father is? I'd like to talk to him."

"That's a change. He and Betsy went to a concert." Betsy was her sister, six or seven years younger. "We can call them this evening."

"Where do you want to meet?"

She chose a place on the West Side in the Fifties.

I locked up and went downstairs. It was 4:30 on a Sunday afternoon, not the best time to hope for a taxicab. I walked up to Broadway. The financial district's warren of Tory-period streets was largely deserted. A few traders, a few maintenance or cleaning people, the workaholics had the neighborhood to themselves. It wasn't really a lonely place. At any point in my walk, I could look up or down Broadway, or along a cross street now and then, and see somebody who had drawn a Sunday shift. There was plenty of light angling from the renovated seaport markets and giving a metallic sheen to buildings that were made of granite.

Plenty of light, a few people within earshot, not really a lonely place. And my sense of being stalked was almost unbearable.

I stopped at Maiden Lane and stared west, at narrow sidewalks descending past a shoe store, a pizza shop, a stationer's, a rapid print shop, past office doorways and bags of trash. There had been a sound down there, and there was no sound now.

Farther up Broadway, Sunday movers were loading a truck. The operation was a long block and a half away. The silence of the street let me hear the bang of a hand truck against a loading step. A man came out of a doorway steering another load of boxes.

This was how it would have looked on Ben Yehuda Street when Yura helped cart the files out of Agritech. So routine and businesslike that everyone who noticed looked the other way.

I watched and felt an urge to run. Utterly idiotic.

Whoever owned the office these fellows were moving had nothing to do with me.

I turned and walked away from them, anyway, toward the foot of Broadway. There was a subway station just outside the courthouse at Bowling Green. I wasn't certain I wanted to go down into the subway, which *would* be lonely, but I knew I wanted to walk. I covered two blocks and the feeling that somebody was staring at the back of my head faded.

My foot left the curb before I heard the car engine. He braked in front of me. A brown face stared at me from the driver's open window. The face had no expression, not even this curiosity. Certainly no malice, which made him unusual in New York even on a Sunday. There was nobody in the backseat. So I asked if he was free to take me uptown.

S*tacy and I* had dinner at Tout Va Bien. We walked the twenty blocks north to her apartment building on Central Park West. My heavily edited account of the last week, broken by Stacy's questions, had taken up most of our dinner talk. By the time she put the coffee on, Charlie had gotten home to his house in Connecticut. I gave him the same version. There was no sign over the phone that he was getting pale and weepy at the thought that I could have been in the line of fire.

He cleared his throat. He was a small dapper man whose voice conveyed almost obsessive orderliness. "Your friend Brickman was up to something. Is that what you think?"

"He was kidding his investors," I said. "How much more he was doing, I'm not sure."

"Does his kidnapping strike you as too convenient?"

"It got Harry out of the way while Agritech's records were cleared out and Levy was murdered. So you could look at it as convenient."

"But not necessarily. They could have hoped to collect a ransom for him. I'm sorry about how it turned out for your friend, Donald, but I can't see what I—"

"There's something you can check out," I said quickly. Beside me, Stacy nodded approval. She didn't care much about Harry Brickman's sins, or his fate. But anything that got me in the habit of dealing with Charlie Kimball was to be encouraged. Connections were her father's specialty. Tracer Minerals kept elected officials' doors open and their cabinet officers smiling.

She took the phone. "This is important, Daddy. Please help."

I didn't hear him sigh. He had too much self-control to express frustration at the inevitable.

"There are two things," I said. "First, does the embassy in Jerusalem think there was more to Agritech than met the eye. Was it a cover for an Israeli government operation?"

He hemmed. "They probably won't know. At best I'll get a guess. On what you've told me, I would say a clandestine involvement isn't likely. They wouldn't have let their own Economic Development people have a visible role."

"It wasn't all that visible."

"It would be visible to people within that ministry. What's the other thing?"

"How serious is the problem with Russian emigré criminals?"

"What do you care how serious it is? Serious enough, obviously."

185

"I just want to know."

"Then I'll ask," he said mildly. His subtext said his daughter's whim sent him on foolish missions, not my curiosity.

After I'd hung up, Stacy asked, "What does any of it matter?"

"It probably doesn't. Except—why did they have to kill Harry? If they'd stolen as much as they could, if they'd cleared out the records, what did Harry matter to them? For that matter, what did the records matter?"

"You said someone else was killed at the same time, an office assistant? Could it have had more to do with her?"

"I don't know," I said. Harry had wondered about her. He'd wondered about Dov Levy. The only one he had ignored was poor Yura, clumsy Yura.

FIFTEEN

Isaiah Stern gave me a hard time the next morning. Had I tried ordering a cheeseburger at the King David? Had I avoided circumcision? Had I noticed the altar in the rear of the El Al planes?

"I slept through morning prayers," I said, hoping he would go back to his office.

"Be careful, my friend. The Master of the Universe notices every slight. Speaking of which, how are your stocks?"

"All right." I was watching a screen full of statistics on Viscount Industries. The company had reported higher profits. The stock had jumped a point on the opening trade. The T-shirt business was on a tear. "How are your stocks?"

"What we should be asking is, 'How are Howard's stocks?' Max has him ensconced down on the sixteenth floor, where he churns out memos on shares that are about to have a big move."

"There was talk of putting him in my office."

"Max would like to replace us all, with the exception of Bradshaw. But if we left, too many of our clients would go with us. Would your people stay and do business with Howard, who would soon be known as Howie, or conceivably Howdie?"

"If Howie cut their commissions, they wouldn't care about his name."

"My clients are more loyal. Most of them attend the Hillcrest Center." Isaiah shrugged. "My immediate interest, apart from your emotional reaction to your trip, is whether you've had time to inspect Howie's memos?"

The southwest corner of my desk had a stack of mail eight miles high. Riffing through it, I'd noticed a strata of one-page notes on Magee & Temple's letterhead. I pointed to the stack, and Isaiah rooted until he found them. "As of Friday afternoon, which is two days after young Howard took his seat downstairs, there had been fourteen of these little bulletins rocketing through the system. Here is one I like. Quote. Fiber Fab Industries' stock is showing strong forward momentum. The shares opened this morning at 103, up from a yearly low of 8. But does the market fully appreciate the potential of Fiber Fab's product line? Aggressive accounts should buy the stock for a short-term move to 115, followed by prices above 200 by year end. H. H. Unquote. The second 'H' stands for Harslip. That came out Friday morning. Friday afternoon, Fiber Fab stock closed at 116. Quite a call, don't you think?"

"The boy's a genius."

"Would it alter your opinion if I told you that ninety percent of Friday's purchases came from Magee & Temple? A stock is up more than twelvefold in a year, and we permit some twenty-one-year-old idiot to say the market doesn't appreciate the company's potential. And then, on that wise word alone, we permit our brokers to push the shares up another thirteen points in a single day. Can you believe it?"

"I doubt we permitted it. We probably encouraged it."

"You're right. And if you check Fiber Fab this morning, you will see the enthusiasm continues. The stock is 120."

He told me the symbol, and I punched it up. "122."

"A couple of his other picks are having big moves, mostly on our buying. If other firms jump on the bandwagon, it can work. Our people can begin selling this afternoon into their buying. Provided their brokers are as gullible as our own. My bet is that Fiber Fab peaks today around 128, wobbles a little tomorrow, and is down ten points on Wednesday. So my brother-in-law is selling it short for me at Merrill Lynch."

He was doing it at Merrill Lynch because Magee & Temple didn't like brokers shorting the firm's best ideas. Unfortunately, with our best ideas, selling them short was the best way to make money. If a stock analyst flipped a coin, he would be wrong only half the time. Our analysts applied more effort and were wrong more often. If they had one that went up, customers agreed to forget the two that went down.

"You're shorting a stock that will be two hundred by year end?" I said in mock disbelief.

"I'm such a fool," he giggled, and went off to sell more.

I called downstairs to our trading desk and bought a thousand Fiber Fab at 122¼ for my own account, called down ninety minutes after that and sold it at 125. As soon as I was out, it jumped to 126½. That was fifteen hundred dollars that could have been in my pocket instead of some other jerk's. But I'd made a few thousand dollars on a loopy stock that could just as easily be trading at half its current price. Nothing to complain about.

I went out and bothered Meg for a while. Timmy Upham was reconciled this week with his wife, which put Meg in an oddly cheerful mood. She was typing a letter that Art planned to send to two hundred chief executives extolling

Magee & Temple's new international bond partnership. Without taking her eyes off the screen, she said, "I guess your desk is safe, Donald."

She chuckled at that, or at its implausibility.

A phone beeped, and she picked it up. "Mr. McCarry's office. . . . I'll see if he's free." Punching the hold button, she resumed typing and said to the computer screen, "Mr. Larkis. Are you in?"

"Tell him I've gone to the dentist."

She punched the line. "Mr. McCarry had an appointment out of the office. Is there a message?"

I couldn't hear anything of the voice on the other end. I remembered it as lacking inflection. He could suggest a felonious set of tax trades in the same flat voice as he described his excessive lust. I wondered how he had proposed to each of his three or four wives. Wondered how he had gotten around his little problem exporting cash.

"I'll see that he gets the message," Meg said and cut him off. She handed a note to me, two fingers over her shoulder, without looking, seemingly without breaking the rhythm of her keystrokes. It had a phone number, Larkis's name, and a two-word message: *re Brickman.*

I crumpled it, pitched it into the trash basket beside her desk. Whatever business Larkis had with Harry's firm, he had none with me.

He called back ninety minutes later, and Meg told him I was still out. After that, I told her to make it an all-day conference. At 4:30, after the market was closed, Charlie Kimball called. He sounded harried with other matters. The answers to my questions were "No" and "Read the newspapers." No, the embassy in Jerusalem didn't think the Israeli government was playing games through Agritech—"except possibly to the extent they play games with everything," he added. The other answer was in response to my question about emigré crime. "My friend says I haven't been reading the newspapers in this country," Charlie said. "There were criminal operations in the old Soviet Union. It went beyond the black economy you would expect to see running vodka and cigarettes. A lot of the more recent immigrant generation have taken it with them where they settled. Not surprising. Chinese, Vietnamese, Colombians, Hondurans, Jamaicans, Italians have all brought the family business to the new homeland. Israel has taken a large percentage of Russian emigrés so it's more noticeable, according to my friend, but per capita it's just as prevalent among those arriving in the U.S." He cleared his throat. "What does that tell you?"

"I don't know. Is your friend on top of things in Israel?"

He gave a dry laugh. "I would say so, Donald." He might have pumped the ambassador himself, except he had probably found somebody better informed a rung or two down the staff.

"Thanks for making the calls," I said.

Somebody was talking to him in the background. He gave a quick yes-yes and said, "I'm happy to oblige. And I'm sorry about your friend. He was playing games with people who are better at it. If I can do anything else. . . ."

We said good-bye.

He *had* been accommodating. He probably did feel bad, in the abstract, about Harry. Since they hadn't known each other, that was all you could ask. Somewhere in the world a friend of a friend is always dropping dead, and you can't keep your handkerchief wet for all those strangers. I wasn't even Charlie's friend.

Meg was gone and I was trading jokes with Isaiah when my line rang again. I picked it up, hoping it was a client wanting to give me hell instead of Gideon Larkis proposing business. It was neither. Ben Ozick asked if I could stop by when I left the office.

"Yes," I said.

There was something in his silence. No banalities about missing Harry, the place not being the same, nothing about the poor widow, or whether she and Morgenstern had returned. Just could I stop by.

So I said yes again.

Ben Ozick was in shirtsleeves, tie askew. He was tall, bald on top, with features set close together as if they'd been designed for a narrower face. He shook my hand, hitched himself onto a desk where he could keep an eye on a computer screen that showed moving prices. The American exchanges were having cocktails but the rest of the world was still at its desk eating corned beef or teriyaki and trading.

"Warren is due back first thing in the morning," Ozick said. "We're getting the auditors in then, too, just to cover our asses. It's a good thing Harry got killed, or I would do the job myself. I hate to go after the widow or the estate, but we've got to try to make everybody we put into Agritech whole. There's a chance it'll blow over with our investors then. We'll have to disclose, but people will look at the numbers first and maybe listen to us tell them it's no big deal."

"How much do you think you're down?"

"If nothing turns up in Israel, two and a half, three million tops. Reduce that by whatever you think they'll recover. Not much, according to Warren. He says it was well planned and slickly executed. He's turned up only about eighteen thousand dollars in the company's bank accounts."

Bad news for people in the field expecting to be paid. I made a sympathetic noise.

Ben Ozick gave me a grim stare. "Warren figures Harry had to be involved in it, in the whole thing. I hate to say it, but it looks bad."

Except to Harry's memory, it didn't matter. Either way, the firm would have to make good.

He saw my expression and said, "You don't agree?"

He meant agree on how deeply Harry was involved.

"I don't agree at all," I said, though I hadn't been thinking about it. "The two schemes are almost mutually exclusive. Harry went to enormous lengths to deceive you and your investors so he could set up the company. He hoped Agritech would be successful, hoped it would benefit Israel in the Third World, but he knew it was chancy. So he got the Israeli government to guarantee the investors' principal plus nine percent. The first is the act of a man carried away with his politics. The second is the act of a man still trying to protect the investors he's deceiving. Neither fits a man who then sets out to wreck the company."

"So we live in a world where being a schmuck gets you killed."

And we were back to my question. Why kill him? Or Esther. I couldn't rule her out as the target. Or Dov Levy? If any or all of them had been involved in looting Agritech, one player might have wanted to eliminate his partners. The urge would be understandable. A couple of million dollars split three or four ways stopped being serious money. The idea that Harry Brickman would loot his creation for a few hundred thousand dollars was absurd. He was probably worth twenty times that amount. To Dov, or Esther, or an outside party, it might be a decade's income. Not to Harry.

To Yura, a lifetime's income. I wondered if Alboker had found him.

Ben Ozick adopted a vague smile, relieved that he only had to think of his partner as a jerk, not as a thief. He said, "You were there. What do you think?"

"The heavy work was done by Russians. If they had an invisible partner, I would start looking for him at the Ministry of Economic Development."

"Warren said there was some junior minister. . . ."

"Yigal Martin."

"What's he like?"

"I never met him. When I left, he was busy renouncing the guarantee to Agritech. Suppose Yigal Martin is corrupt, Harry's abductors haven't lost him, Dov Levy is dead, and Agritech's offices are swept clean. There wouldn't be anyone who knew about the guarantee, except Martin. And Esther Sennesh, but she wouldn't have lasted long."

"What would that have mattered?"

I was groping and knew it. But I liked the fit of the gangs having worked their way into a government ministry. It would be a useful vantage for spotting targets. And hadn't Dov Levy complained that some other agency, involved in immigrant absorption, had foisted Yura Geller on him? But how many ministries and agencies could have been corrupted?

Besides which, what would the fact of the guarantee have mattered?

I answered my own question. "The guarantee led back to the Ministry and Yigal Martin. Without that, no one would have had reason to look in Martin's direction after Agritech failed."

"If he's run the game more than once, someone would notice," Ben Ozick said. "Especially if other people have

194

been murdered. Someone in his own ministry would become alarmed."

"Assuming they know about the guarantee."

"He's taking an enormous risk, if he does the guarantee off the books. My God, one crack, one question asked, and everything falls apart. If I were a bureaucrat looking for companies to rob, I would go after ones I didn't do business with. A lot of companies' proposals must get bounced. Six months, a year later you send your gang after one of them. Who remembers?" His stare left the computer screen. "I don't think it happened that way, my friend. I think it was Harry. But thank you for trying to make me feel better."

I stopped at the door. "Is Gideon Larkis still your lawyer?"

"Until they disbar him. He's Warren's wife's brother."

"He's been trying to call me. Would you tell him to stop? I don't want his business."

"He's got to figure out how we go after Harry's assets. He probably thinks you can help."

"I can't, and I don't like him."

"Neither do I," Ben Ozick said. "He's a lawyer."

Warren *got back* the next morning, called me with perfunctory thanks for my assistance. I hadn't given much and was grateful for the call. He hoped I wouldn't hold it against his firm that Harry had tried to rope me and my clients into a bad situation. He meant he hoped I wouldn't spread the story all over the street. On that score, he had nothing to worry about. Harry had said he hadn't known Agritech was going sour until he saw the accounts. I believed him. He was a jerk, not a thief.

That night—the next morning, really—Karen Brickman

woke me from a sound sleep, screaming hysterically. "They say he stole millions from the firm, *millions!*"

I placed her voice then, though I'd never heard it at that register. So she had gotten the bad news.

"Mrs. Brickman—"

"You're his friend! You know it isn't true! I can't sleep. I can't think. Both Warren and Ben have turned against me. And that dreadful lawyer—!" She gulped. "How can they do this?"

I was awake then, and Stacy was scowling in the pale light from the street as the shrill voice rose in consternation. I said, "Mrs.—Karen—no one is accusing Harry of stealing, exactly. Somebody else stole the money from Agritech. They don't know how much."

"I'm not talking about Agritech! And they do know— they claim they do—it's millions! That miserable goddamned lawyer says eleven million dollars is missing from the firm and Harry stole it."

I was wide awake. *"How much?"*

She repeated herself, and in a crazy way everything made sense. Even to Harry Brickman, eleven million dollars was real money.

"They say he and that Israeli woman were running the money through Agritech. They think the whole thing was set up so Harry could run away with the money." Her voice choked into diminishing sobs. "You know him. You know he wouldn't do that."

He was a jerk. In Esther's bed, he'd have been a jerk who thought he'd died and gone to heaven.

"He *wouldn't*," she said.

"No," I said, and knew better.

SIXTEEN

Warren Morgenstern wore black mourning clothes—for Harry, or the firm, or himself. He looked like a man in his seventies, cheeks sunken under the bones, eyes shiny and blind-looking, skin creased around the mouth as if the shape of skeletal teeth had melted through. Not a well man, you'd have thought. If I'd seen a lifetime's work collapse, I might put on a few years myself. On the other side of a long conference table, Ben Ozick slumped in a chair, staring over everyone's head. I couldn't read anything on his face except perplexity. A man who knew how the world worked might wear that look after being told there was a whole hidden level of rules he hadn't heard about.

Next to Ozick, also in a dark suit, Gideon Larkis was shuffling papers. He was the only one who looked the same as when I'd last met him. His improbably black hair was combed straight back. His long white hands moved with unhurried precision. It was his conference room, in his office on Fifty-fourth Street. He looked up. "What we thought, Mr. McCarry, is that Harold Brickman might have said something, or done something, that in retrospect casts light on this."

I'd been thinking about that. For two hours after Karen's call, I'd thought about Harry and Esther and eleven million dollars. The number had kept me awake. Visions of the hot dry hills north of Jerusalem had finally put me back to sleep.

For most of today I'd found my attention drifting as clients complained about the market. Warren had called at two and asked if we could get together after the market closed. The auditors would have preliminary final figures by then; that was what he called them, "preliminary final figures," and I understood what he meant: final unless more holes appeared in the bottom of Morgenstern Ozick's boat. The audit had turned up a nightmare. His voice on the telephone sounded like a dead man's, reciting words only the living cared about. I'd thought of little since then but Harry and the millions.

Finally you decide you didn't really know him *that* well.

I talked to Charlie Kimball at length at three o'clock, went uptown at five, and waited an hour as the preliminary final numbers were faxed from the auditors at Morgenstern Ozick's office. The tally came to just under nine million dollars that had slipped out of the firm's accounts since the last year-end audit. The method of the theft hadn't been found. The auditors were confident that within a week they would be able to trace every dollar that had moved through every account and learn when and how the money had gone astray. "They will examine wire transfers first," Gideon Larkis said. "That seems the most likely device. Do you agree?"

They were silent, and I held down laughter. *Not a suitcase full of cash, old sport?*

Just under nine million, plus whatever had been sunk into Agritech. Three million more.

Larkis's dry voice prodded. "Anything at all, Mr. McCarry?"

I sagged in my chair, shook my head. "All his talk was about Agritech, and about Israel. He was in an 'On to Damascus' mood."

"If the funds are in Israel, the chances of recovery are small," Larkis said.

Neither of his clients nodded, or winced, or disagreed. His manner was smoother than it had been at the restaurant. I wondered if he'd solved his wife problems. Then he'd been mean and horny. If he hadn't buggered his third or fourth wife in bed, he'd planned to do it in the divorce. Now his rough edges were as far undercover as he probably ever got them. He couldn't do anything about the dark eyes that said you wouldn't leave *your* wife alone with him, or your infant daughter, or a sassy blonde cocker spaniel. He couldn't do anything about a slack white face that suggested he should be sleeping alone, in a coal cellar, with the lid down.

"I don't think Harry had money in Israel," I said.

Warren's glassy eyes tried to focus on me. "No?"

"He was totally preoccupied with Agritech. First with its terrific prospects. Later with suspicions of Dov Levy and Esther Sennesh. By then he knew for sure the company had gone through more money than he could explain. He was looking for a reason. He didn't act like a man with a nine-million-dollar ace in the hole. Or twelve million."

"We must assume, I think, that all of that was a sham," Gideon Larkis said. "There was more to Harold Brickman than met the eye. The partnership's only hope at this point is to find the money he diverted. It's obvious he had accomplices in Israel. He may have had an accomplice in the United States. We will have a better idea when the auditors determine how the money was misappropriated."

"May I ask a question?" I said.

"Of course," Warren said.

"Prior to the audit, had either you or Ben noticed deficiencies in any accounts?"

Before answering, he glanced at Larkis, who nodded. "No, we hadn't," Warren said. "Let me tell you how the firm operates, and you will understand. This is not to excuse negligence, only to explain. Each of us manages a separate pool, of which he is mainly in charge. The three of us jointly invest a fourth, larger pool of money. We measure ourselves against each other, against the common pool, and against the market. Just as you would expect, yes? We all monitor the individual pools, but only for prudence and performance. We wouldn't let one of us get carried away, for example, and violate the firm's rules limiting position size. None of the pools can have more than seven percent of its assets in a single company's securities. We abide by that no matter how much we adore a company, because we have sold the partnership interests to our clients with that restriction in place." Warren settled back. Speaking of the firm's mechanisms as if they weren't anachronisms had revived him only until he remembered the truth.

Gideon Larkis's scowl would have darkened a sunny day. "Cut to the chase, Warren. It was Brickman's pool that came up short. It appears treasury bills were sold by the bank holding them, and the proceeds—" His shoulders gave a tick that might have been a shrug. He didn't know where the proceeds had gone. "Inside this room, I will say the controls at Morgenstern Ozick were deficient—in fact, they sucked."

"You don't have as a partner someone you don't trust," Warren said.

"Your judgment sucked, too," Larkis said. "Apparently the bank statements were intercepted and altered by Brickman. To anyone looking over his shoulder, the treasury bills were still there. It took a line-by-line, statement-by-statement audit to uncover the theft."

"You found him upset about Agritech," Warren said to me. "Now we know why. The exposure that he had deceived people about Agritech was bad enough—"

"It was illegal," Larkis snarled.

"Even if the firm survived that, Harry would be gone. But a breach of faith of *that* dimension—he knew it would force us into a full audit. Then the poor bastard's real crime would come to light. No wonder he was unhappy! He wouldn't dare return to the United States, to Karen and Aaron. You know, Donald, if we could find out what his plans were, find out where he planned to retire, we might know where to look for the money. Not that I'm hoping."

"He liked it where he was," I said. And I thought: *He didn't seem all that ruffled.* If a couple of million was missing, he expected the Ministry of Economic Development to stand behind its guarantee. If he'd technically committed fraud by bringing investors into Agritech under false pretenses, the prospect of being hauled before a court—or pitched into jail—didn't seem to have weighed heavily on his mind. I thought I knew why. Somewhere between his becoming suspicious of Dov Levy and driving back to Jerusalem with Esther and me, he had decided to stay in Israel. He had his little villa, he had a little money, and he had Esther. An Israeli court wouldn't extradite a good Zionist when the people he was accused of defrauding hadn't, when all was said and done, lost anything.

"His accomplices will have stashed that money in a deep hole," Larkis said. "You don't kill people and then leave the marbles where any accountant can find them. Tell me, Mr. McCarry, would you kill people for nine million dollars?"

"No," I said.

"It's a lot of money."

I didn't reply. He was right enough about that. It spilled out income of nine hundred thousand a year. You didn't have to go to the office. You didn't have to clip coupons or go to the racetrack with a paper bag to collect it. That much money bought the owner a different life, and if you thought of yourself as a unique person who deserved the best, somebody standing in the way might become just a jot on the expense ledger. Regrettable, but a cost of doing business.

"You might have thought all you had to do was hide the money," Larkis said.

The bald insinuation didn't shock me. I'd wondered when one of them would get around to it.

"I might have," I agreed. "If I'd been helping Harry steal nine million dollars. If Harry had stolen anything."

Ben Ozick stood up. His hands were trembling. He stuffed them into his trouser pockets. "Harry's dead. That's enough." They were the first words he had said since I arrived.

"Your memory is selective," Larkis said. "It's Brickman, and Levy, and the Sennesh woman."

Ben Ozick nodded in silence. He walked to the door, fumbled with the handle, and closed it behind him.

Warren sighed. "Ben's entire wealth is in the firm. This is killing him."

"Knock it off," Gideon Larkis said. "It's a waste of time. It isn't working."

"Gideon—"

"Be quiet. McCarry was with Brickman in Jerusalem. He

says your partner wasn't sitting on a hill of money. Isn't that right, McCarry?" The nature of the conversation had changed. He switched his attention to the older man. "I told you we might have to deal with this. Don't look so queasy. You were in Jerusalem when your friend got it."

"It's nearly killed *me*," Warren whispered.

"Maybe that should be part of the script," Larkis said. "Ozick ducks out because he hasn't got the stomach for it. You sit and whine. What do you contribute to this?"

"Gideon—"

"Shut up. Go make sure the office is empty."

Warren unfolded himself quickly.

They had spoken as if I weren't there. Not a good sign. Prophetic, maybe.

I got up. Gideon Larkis took a gun from his jacket, set it on the table with a thin hand resting on the grip like a bird. "Sit down," he said. He spoke with no menace, no anger, no bluster, just giving lawyerly instructions. *Sit down, don't be a nuisance.* His casualness about the gun convinced me. He didn't need to point it, wouldn't bother unless he decided to fire.

I supposed I had heard as often as the average person that a handgun is notoriously inaccurate at a distance. This one was an automatic, black like a piece of painted iron, a little larger than a package of cigarettes, with no extended barrel. You couldn't pluck out a gnat's eye at twenty yards, but in a conference room, you wouldn't have to. You could just keep shooting till you hit the right spot.

I backed off a step, sat in a chair farther from him.

Warren came back, and a small bearded man in a brown leather jacket came with him. The man wore snug designer jeans with ostrich hide boots peeking from under the hems. Under the jacket he wore a black T-shirt and several gold chains. He had curly black hair, thin eyebrows, pale blue eyes, a deeply creased forehead, weight-lifter shoulders. Warren Morgenstern shied away. "They're gone," he said. He glanced at me, glanced away.

Gideon Larkis extended a hand. "This is Alexei, Mr. McCarry. A few years ago, I was briefly in the import business. The commodity I brought in was people. Alexei was among the best. Do you find a family resemblance? He is Yura Geller's cousin."

I didn't react.

Alexei came round the table, buttoned my suit jacket and pulled it off my shoulders and down over the back of the chair. The maneuver pinned me as effectively as a few turns of rope.

"Alexei will do whatever I say," Larkis said. "If I tell him to snap your neck, he will do so with no hesitation or compunction but with a professional's economy. If I tell him to kill this weak-kneed fool, poor Warren won't make it to the door. In Minsk, Alexei operated a protection business. I've trained him for more ambitious work. He's quite bright."

"A computer programmer," I said.

"No, that is his cousin's skill. Alexei is an organizer. He has a network of cousins, brothers, in-laws, uncles, nephews, and what-have-yous spread through this country, Russia, and Israel."

"You forget Canada," Alexei said. His voice was throaty, thickly accented.

"And Canada," Larkis said. "We have an informal partnership—I think that's the best description, don't you, Alexei? He certainly doesn't work *for* me."

"I work for myself," Alexei confirmed.

"An entrepreneur in the truest sense."

Warren was standing out of Larkis's sight, shoulders hunched, using the pastel-papered wall for support. He looked ancient and sick.

204

"And I thought Harry was a jerk," I told him.

He nodded but didn't speak.

"Ben, Warren, and I had another investment, a large one, that became a total loss when certain authorities intervened. Having committed more than our own resources," Larkis said, "we had to find a way to recoup. Our partners in that venture are unforgiving."

I could guess the rest. Morgenstern Ozick had access to other people's money. Harry was the outsider. He had an interest in Israel. If they looted the account he managed, it would look like he'd been up to no good at Agritech. He wouldn't be around to set things straight. I said, "Did you decide to kill him right at the start?"

To my surprise, Warren Morgenstern spoke up. "When you find yourself in a tough spot, tough decisions have to be made. There wasn't a choice." He had regained his composure. Against all the evidence, he probably was telling himself he was senior partner in the affair and the maker of tough decisions.

"You were a great convenience," Larkis told me. "You could verify that Brickman had been abducted—by Palestinians, of course. You would be around when the scandal broke at Agritech. But then it started to go bad. Levy had to be dealt with, and Yura took care of that. Brickman's body was supposed to be found next to Levy's. But when your friend escaped, the plausibility of him as thief just wouldn't hold up. As you put it, he didn't act like a man with an ace in the hole. You're a credible witness, unlike his distraught wife. Once you're out of the picture, plausibility returns. Who will dispute that what we say happened?"

"The Israeli police," I said. "People at the embassy."

"All will be content to see the focus shift from their emigré crime problem. An embarrassment for Israel will become an American financial scandal."

205

"Morgenstern Ozick collapses, some investors lose their money, and you boys walk away with full pockets."

"No, we walk away almost broke, but alive," Larkis said. "When our debts are paid, there will be only enough left for Alexei. But we can start again."

"I haven't got the *time* to start again," Warren protested.

"You haven't got a choice." Larkis stared at him with distaste. "What I need to know from you, McCarry, is whether you shared your high opinion of Brickman with anyone else. Alexei will help you remember."

Standing behind me, Alexei swept the heel of his hand across my head. Rocks bounced around in my skull. When I focused on anything again, it was on Warren Morgenstern leaning against the wall, looking unhappy. He'd gone from being the maker of tough decisions to a man too old to start again.

"Let's start with your friends," Larkis said. "Who is close to you—someone you *might* have told?"

I said, "No one," and Alexei hit me.

"Take as long as you like," Larkis said as my vision cleared. "Alexei has patience. Who are your friends?"

"Stockbrokers have clients, not friends."

That bit of candor earned me another blow. I sagged forward, held by my jacket. Alexei had started using a fist— that or a chair leg. The pain was too widespread for me to be certain, but I thought each blow had struck the same spot. It seemed altogether possible that Alexei, given his patience and enough time, could pound a hole through a man's skull.

"Do you know his friends?"

The question floated in some world apart from me. Was I supposed to answer? Or Alexei? It was Warren's voice that came. "I'm trying to think. Harry mentioned a girlfriend with a lot of money. The name didn't mean anything."

"Do you talk business with your girlfriend?"

When I didn't answer, Alexei shook my shoulder.

I said, "What?"

"Do you talk business with Miss—what's her name?"

"Kimball," I said thickly.

"Kimball—that was it!"

"Did you tell her about Harry?"

"Not her. . . ."

"Someone else?"

Alexei coaxed me by hitting the same spot. I rocked forward, retching.

"Someone else?"

I said something so strangled they couldn't understand.

Gideon Larkis said, "Go easy on him for a moment. I think he wants to tell us."

Alexei's rough hands pulled me upright. They lingered on my shoulders like a comforting friend's.

"Who else?" Larkis said.

My tongue didn't want to move. Alexei had hit me harder, I thought, than Larkis realized. The hands squeezed my shoulders, assuring me everything could be all right.

I said, "I told your third wife, or the fourth one . . . the one you like to bugger."

After that, Alexei lost his patience.

"If *you hit* him too hard—"

"If he did, he did. No, he's breathing. Mr. McCarry—Donald—it's important you answer my questions. You need medical attention, which we can arrange as soon as this is done. Alexei is becoming difficult to control. He wants to go home to dinner."

The voice was a pinpoint in darkness. I wondered if Alexei had hit me so hard or so often that I was blind. I opened my eyes, and Warren Morgenstern's face swam into view. Into view, but not into focus. Even with fuzzy edges, Warren looked as sick as I felt. He was leaning across the table, mouth slack, eyes wide. There was a bad smell nearby, which turned out to be the front of my vomit-soaked shirt.

"Are you feeling better?" Gideon Larkis hadn't moved from his chair.

I summoned as much coherent thought as I could and said, "What time is it?"

"What do you care about the time?"

"Dinner. . . ."

"Oh, you want to go to dinner, too?"

I didn't dare nod. I groaned assent.

"He's concussed, delirious," Warren said.

"No, he's feeling better, aren't you, Donald? It's 6:20. We'll all go to dinner soon. You were remembering a name for me. Somebody that you talked to that I could talk to. Remember?"

If I didn't answer now, I knew, Alexei really would kill me. I licked my lips, tasted vomit. I shaped the name, forced it out. "Charlie Kimball."

"Kimball. What did you tell him?"

"I told him I didn't think Harry Brickman was a thief."

Gideon Larkis seemed to be considering. "Is that all? Did you give him any reasons?"

"Not exactly. . . ."

"Not exactly?"

"I said I liked Harry." I wanted more than anything else to stay awake. "And I told him I thought you were a crook. You and Morgenstern."

Larkis ignored Warren Morgenstern's groan. He asked in a mild, lawyerly tone, "Now why would you have said that?"

"I told you. Harry wasn't a crook. There were only three choices. Harry, Warren, or Ben. And you. And I knew you were a sleaze. That part was easy. But I wasn't sure whether it was you, you and Warren, or all three of you."

"And you told this to . . . Kimball." His smooth, deposition-taking manner had cracked.

Having sicced them on Kimball, I decided to decorate the cake. "I also told a very bright young man at my firm, Howard Harslip. And the office manager, Max Oberfeld. And—"

"He's enjoying himself," Warren gasped. He leaned heavily on the table, face darkening. "He's— he's told—" Words clotted in his throat. "We're— going— to have— to ahh—"

He straightened, raising a hand to his forehead. He took a heavy step backward. His next step missed the carpet and he bumped a chair, tilted, grabbed it with both arms, and pulled it over onto himself. For a moment he was sitting on the floor, eyes and forehead visible across the table. Then he sank out of sight against the wall.

Gideon Larkis stood up and looked.

I tried to stand. Alexei's hands suppressed me.

"He's having a heart attack," I said. I'd seen a grandfather turn that color.

Larkis ignored me.

"You could call an ambulance."

Larkis didn't respond.

"You could apply CPR." I couldn't hear even a sound of breathing from the other side of the table.

"I'm afraid I'm not familiar with the procedure," Larkis said.

"I am."

"But this way is so much better."

He made a gesture, and Alexei lifted me out of the chair.

From that vantage I could watch the old man die. His face was purple, eyes bulging, mouth shaping silent round gulps.

Larkis kept watching long after there was nothing to see. He pointed and I bounced into the chair. He said, "In a sense you killed Warren. The thought of all those people knowing—what would we do about them? But you weren't telling the truth, were you? I don't think you were. I don't think you said anything definite to any of those people. Perhaps nothing at all. Am I right?"

I didn't answer.

"In fact, I think all we have to do is remove you and our problem is solved."

"People knew I was coming here. People downstairs saw me arrive."

"And you left these law offices and who knows what misadventure befell you after that?"

He was getting close to doing something. I cried: *"I told Charlie Kimball everything!"*

"You're pleading, like a coward. Alexei—"

The door behind his shoulders opened. Charlie Kimball inspected the scene. A gray-haired black man beside him pointed a shotgun at Gideon Larkis. Other men came in fast. Charlie pointed to me, saying, "Don't shoot that one."

Gideon Larkis lifted a hand away from his gun. "What is the problem?"

"No problem, Mr. Larkis," said the man with the shotgun. "Letting that man die, while restraining a Good Samaritan who offered to help, that looks awfully close to murder. You're under arrest."

SEVENTEEN

An *emergency room* doctor decided that either I was mildly concussed or I had shingles. She confided that neither would impair the depredations of a stockbroker, wrote me a prescription, and cut me loose. Outside the door, Charlie Kimball was waiting, legs crossed, in somebody else's wheelchair.

As he sprang up, I said, "You were supposed to have crashed in ten minutes earlier."

"Oh—well, what was the key word?"

"Bugger."

He chuckled. "I told the captain we'd misheard. You were getting such fine stuff."

He was impressed with himself, pleased he had been able to get a pocket transmitter for me and attract the interest of a notoriously bureaucratic police department on short notice. It helped that he mentioned Gideon Larkis. A deputy commissioner knew Larkis and disliked him.

"Just imagine," Charlie said, "if you'd gone to all that trouble and your hunch had been wrong."

"Just imagine if you and your captain had sat around a few minutes longer. You'd have had two corpses."

His daughter hurtled down the corridor, spotted us, and rushed over. She inspected me and frowned at the absence of wounds or bandages. "You said he was *hurt*," she told her father. Not really disappointed, but pretending.

"He was complaining to anyone who would listen."

A police detective in a blue tweed jacket joined us. He said his name was Taliafaro. "Morgenstern was dead at the scene. Ozick we arrested back at his office. Neither he nor Larkis has anything to say."

"And Alexei?" Charlie said.

"Alexei has nothing to say. He has no papers, at least not on him, and one of the things he's not saying is where he lives." When Charlie wasn't looking, he watched him with a speculative frown. The little gray-haired man wasn't a cop, didn't hold a title in any of officialdom's quasi-police ranks, and yet he had been able to scramble a platoon of officers, of whom Taliafaro was one.

Stacy was more impressed. She admired Charlie Kimball lavishly, tried not to let it show, failed often. Charlie was a master of getting people to do things. Stacy couldn't get a sort-of fiancé to settle down and work for Daddy.

"You captured them *all?*" she cried, addressing her father and ignoring the policeman.

"The police did the capturing," he said.

"But you led them to the criminals?"

"Donald had something to do with that."

She was in the middle of a this-can't-be look when her father put a hand on her shoulder. "Let's take Donald home."

In the taxi, I filled Charlie in as much as I could on the scheme.

He listened. "It was about what you thought. Remarkably shrewd guesswork."

He paid compliments the way he paid taxes, four times a year unless he could get by on less. I hated to turn back praise I might never hear again. "It wasn't shrewd," I said. "I didn't think Harry was guilty. I tried, but it just didn't work. That didn't limit the field much in Israel. I was half-convinced the deputy minister of Economic Development had a hand in looting Agritech. Or Dov Levy, or a woman who worked with him."

"Miss Sennesh," he said. Our eyes met briefly across Stacy, and I wondered who he had been talking to in Israel. Another of Charlie Kimball's talents was learning other people's secrets.

"Yes, Miss Sennesh," I said. "But that didn't hold together even before they were killed. The people who hijacked Harry weren't Arab, he said. He hadn't heard them speak; why was that? The fellow he hit when he got away looked as if he could have been Israeli, even in the army. But Israelis have come from all over, so that didn't say much. From Harry's description, the man could have been Russian. If you spoke with a heavy Russian accent, you wouldn't talk around a captive. When Agritech's files were removed, their own Russian, Yura, was helping. So I was inclined to think the looting of Agritech occurred largely from the outside, with Yura as a plant. When Karen Brickman told me last night that money was missing from Morgenstern Ozick as well, it was too much coincidence. Yura and his fellow emigrés in Israel couldn't have done that. The obvious common denominator was Harry Brickman."

Charlie picked up the thought. "You either had to revise your opinion of Brickman or find another common denominator."

"Warren was almost as easy a candidate as Harry."

"Except that Warren hadn't lured investors into Agritech under false pretenses."

"There I had to make a distinction," I said. "Was Harry a thief or just a jerk?"

Stacy got out of the cab with me at SoHo, saying even an Irish head could use a cold compress. Charlie declined my offer of a drink and drove off.

We went upstairs, turned on the lights, started a tea kettle.

"One question," Stacy began, and my shoulders clenched. It would be about Esther Sennesh, and I was too tired to lie. She said, "How would Mr. Morgenstern and Mr. Larkis have gotten Yura a job at Agritech?"

"Maybe a well-placed bribe at the immigrant absorption agency," I said, not caring. The thought of government agents taking bribes left her looking scandalized.

I was looking through tall, iron-columned windows down to the street, which was beginning to sprout its evening decorations. The scene of indulgent, apprehensive idiocy was as familiar to me as the apartment, or the suite at Magee & Temple, or the measures of this woman's temper. The smells of an orange grove and Esther were receding. The stockbroker's instinct was asserting itself. You had to forget the losers.